'A work of reflective intensity, re-imagining a memorable character from JM Coetzee's world of stark and sparse prose and transplanting him in Mohlele's ornate and lyrical one. Told mostly in a restrained register and with direct characterisation that consciously distances the reader emotionally, the work glistens with humour and a delightful turn of phrase. Mohlele pays homage to Coetzee by appropriating and subverting Coetzee's tools of metafiction and intertextuality to provide his own closure to *Life and Times of Michael K*.'

Zakes Mda

MICHAEL K

MICHAEL K

Nthikeng Mohlele

PICADOR AFRICA

First published in 2018 by Picador Africa
an imprint of Pan Macmillan South Africa
Private Bag X19, Northlands
Johannesburg, 2116

www.panmacmillan.co.za

ISBN 978-1-77010-479-2
eBook ISBN 978-1-77010-587-4

This book is a work of fiction. Any resemblance to actual places or persons, living or dead, is purely coincidental.

Editing by Sean Fraser
Proofreading by Kelly Norwood-Young
Design and typesetting by Fire and Lion
Cover design by K4
Cover image © Shutterstock (Rural landscape with a farm in engraving style)
Author photograph © Oupa Nkosi, courtesy of the *Mail & Guardian*

Printed and bound by

ALSO BY NTHIKENG MOHLELE

Pleasure (2016)

Winner of the 2016 University of Johannesburg Main Prize for
South African Writing in English

Winner of the 2017 South African Literary Awards K Sello Duiker
Memorial Literary Award

Longlisted for the 2018 International Dublin Literary Award

'You have to have a gift with words to paint so effortlessly what
Mohlele captures about Milton's angst, fears and rebellion.'
– Mapula Nkosi, *Sowetan*

'*Pleasure* is a galloping linguistic trip. It is packed with sharp and
often poignant visual sketches and it touches on many matters of
serious moment, such as racism and poverty in South Africa.'
– David Pike, *The Witness*

'Loaded with vivid but delicate passages and complex situations,
Mohlele's latest novel is an ambitious exploration of pleasure
beyond its superficial interpretations.'
– Kwanele Sosibo, *Mail & Guardian*

'*Pleasure* is a mesmerising, unusual book. At times I was hesitant to
call it a novel. The story of Milton Mohlele, his dreams and
musings, which he attempts to distil into writing, reads like a
meditation.' – Karina M Szczurek, *Cape Times*

Rusty Bell (2014)

'*Rusty Bell* is an intricate exploration of love, fate, lust, death and grief … illustrating that the light is not the place for answers, because sometimes they are visible only from the shadows.'
– Lloyd Gedye, *The Con*

Small Things (2013)

'Behind this story of love, music and the eternal quest lies an artistic sensibility as generous as it is complex. The prose is rich in texture, the final effect melancholy and comic in equal proportions.'
– JM Coetzee

The Scent of Bliss (2008)

'An outstanding poetic piece of work … Mohlele's voice is novel and shows a concern … for beautiful language for its own sake.'
– Percy Zvomuya, *Mail & Guardian*

For my wife, Sharon Mohlele, for everything she does for me.

And for Naledi Mohlele, the brightest star in my firmament, and Miles Mohlele, the best friend one can ever wish for.

Also for my dearest friend and mentor, Professor Keorapetse Kgositsile – thank you for your laughter and wisdom.

JOHANNESBURG

A man I have known all my life, all fifty-three years, one I have loved, admired and revered, a man of impeccable manners and good humour, Maurice M, my father, walked into my study around 6 pm, handed me a loaded Smith & Wesson and implored me to shoot him in the head. What does one say to such a request, so sudden and final? I had, until that moment, never held a gun in my hand, the cold and ruthless instrument designed for the sole purpose of populating cemeteries. It was the manner of the request, like nothing ever existed before it, nothing after: just that permanent, forceful, draining imposition. That was a year ago, but does not mean I have not been permanently disfigured by the memory. I woke up in hospital that evening, plugged into beeping machines. Alcohol poisoning.

Shoot me in the head: a polite and whispered request for the bloodying of hands, the splattering of walls. People are of course entitled to request anything they please, even daunting things, things that impose shock and bewilderment in those asked. It was not so much that Father made the ultimate request – perhaps the greatest test of love and loyalty, of empathy – but rather that a part of me was so tempted, even half reconciled, to pick up the pistol, aim, close my eyes and pull the trigger.

Euthanasia? No, it would not have been that. Maybe an expression of frustration, of despair, of helplessness in witnessing the indignities suffered by my father. It was, for a man of his stature, reputation, a man of his resolve, heartrending to witness his lapses in composure, his embarrassing excesses, his oblivious submission to a decaying body. I nursed him, stroked his back, reassured him of my love and what remained of his imploding dignity. Disease does that to you: strips you of composure, robs you of hope, renders everything urgent but impossible. You know and are reminded of lurking death: doctors tell you that; shocked faces of friends confirm it, and yet there is nothing to be done to change anything. The intermittent outbursts of violence, the insults and rages, the trouser-wetting and tearful meltdowns. The refrain from doctors and relatives was the same: he is not himself. For safety and practical reasons, I had, because of a blue eye he gave me during one of his sudden rages before he was wheelchair-bound, when he could still walk, resorted to securing him on a dog leash, walking him like a hound. I guess I had simply grown tired of him getting lost, of reporting him missing, searching for weeks, assuming him dead, only for him to resurface in some obscure hospital, sceptical and morose.

My father was a good-looking man, handsome almost; educated, deeply religious, and an ardent admirer of both John F Kennedy and Lyndon B Johnson – a glaring contradiction, I know. He was not into what he called 'home politics', and spent considerable time reading about the Bay of Pigs, piles of political biographies, from Mandela to Sergeyevich Khrushchev. Churchill too. Winston, he famously said once, was the most emotive and passionate of politicians, living or dead. So I grew up listening to countless recordings of historic addresses played from morning till mid-afternoon, paused at meal-times, during which my father would recite Kennedy's *Ich bin ein Berliner* with pride and gusto.

There was very rarely music in our house, just political speeches in various guises: UN meetings, presidential addresses, famous remarks to the press by Henry Kissinger, arguments and counter-arguments from high-profile political court cases and Commissions of Inquiry. We knew without being told who it was who said, '*Lass' sie nach Berlin kommen*', though we had no idea what a Boston accent was. We kept the company of Gandhi and Castro, swam to the majestic speeches of Dr King lamenting the age of war and the rise of machines, to Patrice Lumumba opining about liberty and prosperity.

Mother, who was Wits University's most accomplished historian, would mock my father behind his back, sneer at his favourite utterances, including one we found hilarious, when he would assume presidential posture and gestures, saying: 'General Secretary Gorbachev, if you seek peace, if you seek prosperity for the Soviet Union and Eastern Europe, if you seek liberalization, come here to this gate. Mr Gorbachev, open this gate. Mr Gorbachev, tear down this wall!' Mother said the man Father tried to impersonate was Ronald Reagan, an American president whose reputation – good or bad? – historians and economists can't agree on. She said the speech had been made at the Brandenburg Gate in West Berlin on June 12 of 1987. I did not know what the Brandenburg Gate was, or where it could be found.

From that old Blaupunkt stereo the world's leaders, living and dead, spoke: threatened, reassured, warned, cautioned, despaired, triumphed and surrendered, made estimations and commitments to fortitude, mapped and hid affairs of state in their glory and gore. I warmed to the gifts of oratory, to mundane and moving speeches that made my ceremonial father reserved and emotional, affairs of state that sounded powerful but had little or no meaning. Churchill was Churchill, Kennedy Kennedy, but I was hard-pressed to understand why they never tired of talking, why – according to Mother – they wanted different things, that it was important for the world to know what they thought, what they stood for, that for which they were prepared to die: presidents, prime ministers, envoys, names and voices my ceremonial father knew and Mother mastered, events my ceremonial father touched on but which Mother knew backwards, famous utterances my ceremonial father misinterpreted but Mother comprehended. There were glaring distinctions to be made between my ceremonial father with presidential ambitions and Mother, the highly decorated historian. The historian knew the speeches, the meetings and arguments that led to the speeches, the key players who dictated matters from the shadows, from the blind spots of history. She knew the quips, the miscalculations, the secret ambitions of deceased speechwriters, politicians and their mistresses, the unintended outcomes of unpredictable happenings. Mother humanised history. Hers was not just citations of people and dates, of documents and archives, obscure references to periods and places, but flesh-and-blood individuals who steered events, said important and puzzling things that culminated in broadcasts from my ceremonial father's stereo. Mother was of course interested in the fact that Abe Lincoln abolished slavery, but was equally fascinated by and invested in the fact that he was a manic depressive, that he was never once photographed alongside his wife, that he wore size-fourteen shoes. History, said Mother, is written by men and women of conscience, not by historians and television cameras. The purest history, cautioned Mother, existed in the hearts of those touched by words and events rather than in newspapers and libraries. That even at its vaguest, its most contradictory, its most impassioned, history suffered a multitude of fatalities: its wrestling with the present, its defencelessness against fading memory, its uneasiness when faced with scrutiny.

But, while Mother was a pragmatic idealist with a bent for rationale, Father was a romantic, albeit a cautious one, one who shunned pragmatism for philosophy, theory for action. He shunned convention, shrugged off society's rules as often he did his clothes. He was, as nudists go, not one of the brightest or most imaginative. He was certainly no Larry Flynt, not one of those supple young men photographed nude in horse stables or cow sheds, muscular men dipped in glistening oil with a rose between their teeth. Father was not that kind; never was. He was, at seventy-three, not what you would call stable either, even though I knew other seventy-three-year-olds with a full command of their senses. Dementia is a merciless thing, I tell you, and combined with grief, it reduced my father to a shirtless or trouserless wanderer around the house: bending, squatting, or stretching his aged self in search of unknowable things. There was nothing worse than being confronted by one's nude father at the breakfast table, who unaware of his state of undress still issued instructions: 'No one in this house must ever come to the breakfast table without taking a bath. Family tradition,' and could, when not a soul stirred, continue unfazed.

What time is it anyway?

Where is your mother?

Mom is deceased, Papa, remember? I would answer.

When? He would ask, wide-eyed and startled.

Seven years now.

What happened?

An overgrown ovarian cyst that ruptured, Papa, I would explain again. I told and reminded you of this seven hundred times already. Okay, the latter I wouldn't say out loud.

He would tear up: Oh.

It was difficult to tell where the dementia started and ended, when his head injury from a vehicle accident took over, when grief insisted on being present. Sad, because Father had been one of the happiest people I have ever known.

I live a colourful life. Even for a bachelor. Well, almost. I am not someone you would consider important, not readily noticeable, am coy and somewhat reclusive. I don't think of myself as shy, yet am often misread as such. My soul bleeds, though, pruned by zealots and charlatans with blunt tools, butchered by souls with stale breath and unkempt nails, slashing with questionable sobriety while agitated, in a hurry to fondle their lovers. I am, as specimens of madmen go, educated, urbane, some morals cast in concrete. I suffer certain addictions: coffee and carrot cake for sure, but also petite women with bed-warming tendencies. I adore rain, am friendly to pets – but only of the hygienic kind – and loathe chewing gum and public toilets. I am aware of my ripening madness, the dashes of rarer and profounder contortions of lunacy imposed on me by the grand madness of our age. It must be pointed out, however, that mine is not a madness of the mind, but a volatility of a fragile heart, a heart that has never learnt the raw power of seductions of the conventional kind.

DUST ISLAND

There is a dot on the horizon – or, more precisely, a dot on the long dirt road that bisects the distant mountains, cutting across the plains mocked by worthless shrubbery to the west and teased by the promise of farming to the east. Here is a cold fact: proper farming is impossible here. The weather is too temperamental, too volatile, making hard labour and the prospects of a worthwhile harvest precarious. And yet a paradox remains: farm or perish. The rains can be good, but never reliable, because the storms can be so obscene and dictatorial that it is often pointless even to live in hope. Last night saw such a display of the arrogance of nature – first just the hint of a breeze, a stirring, then a whirlwind that morphed into a brief dust storm, and an unexpected hailstorm overnight. The relief from the sweltering heat turned to worry and finally terror when the storm seemed determined to snuff out the light and nudge the devil even closer to Dust Island, a seemingly forgotten outpost far flung from Cape Town.

All around there is evidence of how ill mannered storms here can be: amputated trees, ravaged birds' nests, savaged vegetable gardens, cracked and broken windowpanes. The wet earth, crimson, makes it impossible to know for certain if that dot is in fact a figment of my imagination. The heat brings with it discomforts of varied kinds, but also certainty, in that dots on the horizon can be confirmed to be moving objects – a truck or motor car raising clouds of dust. Donkey carts do not do that; neither does the postman on horseback every third week. You have to be either remarkably stupid or a spiritual crusader to exist on this frontier, with its dried-up dams and rusted windmills, its abandoned ostrich farms and neglected piggeries. It is doubtful whether God intended Dust Island for human habitation – or whether its harshness was simply a refusal to be settled, farmed. There is a sense of progressive but hesitant decay about the place, which perhaps explains the trickling in of nomads and fugitives, as well as reticent D-grade novelists dabbling in philosophy at solitary retreats, moral castaways courting obscure lives.

We buried Jimmy Hendricks yesterday – a burial before the storm, laid to rest one of our greatest luminaries, understood to be and acknowledged as a talented poet, even though none of the Dust Islanders have read a single stanza by him. He was blind and senile, great by reputation. Some opined that poetry resided in every flutter of his eyelids, each curl of smoke from his pipe, in the raw passion with which he dug graves. It is not a fancy cemetery, the

Twelve Apostles, the graves more heaps of red earth than the mosaics and cathedrals of Cape Town. We know who is buried where – the modest graves given distinction by means of thorn wreaths, motor-oil cans and rusted saucepans, crosses cobbled together from firewood and rope.

There is, in this outpost of low-lying shrubs and anthills with not a single butterfly in sight, the devastation of our burials and sombreness of our weddings. We live by a generally accepted principle that each household, no matter how debased or fragile, is expected to master a trade. So there are coffin makers, coffee-bean purists, gravediggers (day or night, rain or shine), brewers of trusted home remedies. We scout for Jimmy Hendricks's poetry in outlying caves – carved into tree trunks, chiselled on defunct tractor ploughs. But wasn't poetry supposed to be abundant, in plain sight, not obscure? Or did writing it in blood on his donkey cart give his work literary tremors, artistic worth? Dust Island legend has it that there was a time that Poet Hendricks wrote devastating poetry in long hand, rhyming prose committed to the back of matchboxes – verse that travelled back and forth among Dust Island's thirty households, as Dust Islanders borrowed and returned as few as three matchsticks. The very being, the essence and integrity of Dust Islanders included returning seven matchsticks if seven had been borrowed, on time and free of defects. Late or defective matchsticks could plunge a household into darkness render cooking impossible, strain relations. The same applies to salt and paraffin – to ensure bearable food and lit lanterns.

No one knows for sure where the dirt road originates, only that it is long and old, as old as the weather and the seemingly time-proof fence that borders it, a fence afflicted by rust and minor acts of vandalism (a piece stolen to fix a broken shoe or a wheelbarrow, to replace a pot handle). The fence tells silent stories – stories only Dust Islanders seem to understand: how it whistles when a breeze warns of looming whirlwinds; alarming confirmations of the presence of deadly serpents that have shed their skins along the perimeter – how the discarded skin flutters, recoils and straightens in the wind with potentially deadly insignificance; and that the beginning of rotting wooden posts indicates another two hours' walk to the R403, which by bicycle or truck leads to the N2 into Cape Town. Every walk or bicycle trip to the R403 is understood to be suicidal: lightning strikes, snakebites, the pounding of hailstones the size of fat peaches. The happenings of Cape Town are distant and hazy, those daring enough to brave unpredictable thunderstorms in the summer telling of road signs pinpointing only the general direction of the city. Cape Town is another world, foreign and mystical, existing without any sense of immediacy.

About all I knew of Cape Town and its surrounds, though still sketchy and fragmented, was from my neighbour of just over eleven months, a tall scrawny man with a harelip, who spoke with a fully formed lisp. An avid pumpkin gardener, he claimed to have had survived a war and a stint at a hospital, that he had worked as a gardener in his youth – evident in how he handled gardening tools. He spoke rarely and dispassionately about Anna K, his deceased mother, who perished on a wheelbarrow trip to Prince Albert. In blue overalls my neighbour tended to his pumpkin seedlings, taking great care to remove even the most harmless weed that dared invade the spotless garden, cultivated and watered with deep and practised tenderness.

The rest of his story emerged as little more than disjointed fragments, lost amid what seemed like meditative withdrawals. He was the only Dust Islander without any sense of communal belonging – lonesome and solitary. He could not be accused of being arrogant or unpleasant, though. We had come to respect that he lived in his own world and, when it wasn't pumpkin season, spent most of his days slumbering in the shadow of a tree or gazing forlornly into the distance. It was evident that he had had a hard life – but not one bludgeoned by matrimonial fallouts, not one distorted by debt or the perils of disease. It could be concluded that he was, except for the harelip and skew nose, not a sickly man. And yet, a peculiar weariness wore him down, such that he existed rather than lived among other Dust Islanders. He could not be accused of laziness either, for he could be quite industrious, committed to ferrying water in buckets or chopping wood to the point of exhaustion. Or maybe it was the ongoing construction: dislodging a stone here, plucking a hole there, and sealing defects with laborious patience. But then weeks could go by without him even emerging from his house – a single-window pyramid impression cast from wood and mortar that had miraculously withstood Dust Island storms. Impromptu visits found Michael K sprawled on his bed, his breathing shallow, fast asleep. It was a constant source of amazement how someone could sleep day and night without stirring – fully clothed in blue overalls, nibbling on raw pumpkins in between, leaving rabbit-like bite marks on the vegetable, spitting seeds out onto the floor as insurance for subsequent harvests. As seed banks go, Michael K had the most impressive collection in all of Dust Island, seeds categorised and stored in see-through peanut-butter jars and old Coca-Cola bottles. Peaches. Spinach. Avocados. Mealies. Pumpkins. And watermelons.

Not unexpectedly, Michael K was a source of some curiosity, or perhaps it was just me. What does the *K* in your name stand for, I asked him, to which he shrugged his shoulders and continued nibbling on a piece of pumpkin. Was it an initial, a nickname or the first letter of a last name – Koekemoer, for instance, or Kloete? I persisted, but he just mused and walked away.

One could say he was an old man – not only because of earthly years, but soul old. There was a distant knowing in his eyes, ever-shifting calculations on how to exist with the least amount of effort and interpersonal entanglements. There was evidence – unreliable, admittedly – that he had perhaps been a smoker once, but the stained teeth could have been no more than poor dental hygiene, his constant excavations into uncooked pumpkins. There was no doubting that Michael's life belonged entirely to him, his opinions or expectations entirely his own: how he related to work and sleep, how he burrowed in that skew pyramid of his – skew like his nose – into which one had to crawl on all fours. Besides raw pumpkins, Michael K derived great pleasure from overripe watermelons – a remarkable and disgusting culinary display in which he buried his entire face into the fruit, made sucking sounds, and rose with melon water dripping to his chin, doing its best to conceal the inner workings of that afflicted mouth, which bore the obscenities of half-chewed watermelon. It puzzled, intrigued and bothered me how anyone could survive on erratic gougings of vegetables and fruit, on meditative slumber for days on end. How was it that Michael K remained so fragile, yet so present, so imposing without attempting to be so? He wasn't exactly a nuisance, an irritant worth strangling, because he kept to himself, existed without any apparent interest in Dust Island and its modest funerals, its laborious church sermons and tacky weddings – including one where the bridegroom had questionable if not downright dirty fingernails.

Those in the know claim Michael K disembarked from a diesel-smoke-spewing truck one overcast morning, looked around, and without missing a beat, chose a spot where he set down a small bucket (red, burnt and disfigured) that contained an assortment of seedlings, some fisherman's twine and a rudimentary gardening tool – probably self-made. The twine had marked two small portions of garden, about thirteen paces in length and four in breadth. No one knows for sure where he slept. He wandered along the perimeter fence in the purgatorial sun, assessing and collecting things: firewood, discarded food cans, tree bark, thorny shrubs, rusted windmill blades. Some rocks, too, that when forced into an unexpected union yielded the pyramid with chaotic design. It lacked aesthetic credentials, yes, but was built strong, with corrugated-iron sheeting to deflect rain and dust storms. A room for one: a pyramid-like tomb with interlocking logs for a door. Two old saucepans, their bases rusted away to leave only the rim, took care of a view that from the inside looked like badly designed binoculars. Three logs, dried stems of trees that died young, were arranged in triangular form and padded with fresh leaves: K's sleep and meditation throne.

I often wondered what Anna K would have thought of her son were she still alive; his solitary ways, his inventiveness; finding elementary solutions to the complex problems of making life only just comfortable; his admirable skill in preserving energy and emotions. What do mothers of such beings think, if anything? Are such sons just that – sons, nothing more? Or is there secret weeping and silent prayers that the world not be too brutal to them? It is not unbearable or unreasonable to think that Anna K would, even when assailed by swollen legs and a wheezing chest, have yearned to cuddle a grandchild while aware that such yearnings were stillborn; that a specimen like Michael was perhaps never intended for procreation; that such earthly preoccupations never crossed life radars of such higher-born mammals as Michael K; that the connections and dictates of heritage and civilisation mattered little to such sons, born with obscure preoccupations of their own. Could it be that Anna K herself came from a long lineage of disconnected and unaffected ancestors – mute helping hands in the households of others, charity cases at the mercy of the generosity and pity of nuns, nurses and other strangers? Could Michael, seemingly dazed and otherworldly, be trusted in attesting that Anna K groaned with pain and the cold in her last days? Didn't she find it touching, albeit inadequate, that the very best her son could offer to counter her aches and gloom was a wheelbarrow ride around the block – for some fresh air? Had the Michael Ks of the universe figured out the elusive, the great and the profound – that an escape from the stuffiness of borrowed lodgings, the confinement of four walls reeling with anxieties, was a much weightier gesture than siring offspring?

The arrival of Michael K in Dust Island, the history says, put in doubt and question the sequence and motives with which people do things (Michael K thought it important to prioritise a vegetable garden over shelter, and when he did give lodging some thought, did so in so foreign and distorted a manner that his pyramid became a source of ridicule and wonder – an object of great power and disbelief, a spit in the faces of time and the universe), the sheepish ways with which they ponder assaults on happiness and freedom.

Though it was never confirmed with any measure of certainty or comparative estimations, it did become apparent that K's burrowing and seventeen-hour siestas were not merely vacuums of idleness. There seemed to be a hazy pattern in his languid gaze, a hint of mind-bending ideas that resisted forcefulness, ideas that presented only shadows of other ideas, which dissolved into each other as soon as they took shape, leaving a trail of suspicious weightlessness. Bushy-armpit Michael splashing water in the moonlight, almost purring at the pleasure of a soapless rainwater bath in feeding troughs intended for goats; the indifference with which he let water drip down his generous gift of testicles that could have sired an entire generation of watermelon-worshipping simpletons. But opinions were varied: some dismissed him as a vagabond whose mind had long since fused, others that he was born ahead of his time; I, in turn, remained intrigued and confused. A bony body bathing in the moonlight, once every three weeks or so, to lie on a bed of fresh leaves, the rich brown hair greying in parts, ironed back with open palms to reveal a resilient forehead, eye sockets housing dim eyes, eyes that could flicker to life in a nanosecond, or lie hazy and dormant for weeks on end.

It came as no surprise, then, that Michael's solitary life, his pre-dilection for quiet and contemplation, his lone ramblings across veld and garden, eyes averted heavenward, were cause for gossip and speculation. There were rumours that Henrietta, the widowed daughter of Dust Island's much-revered reverend, tip-toed to Michael K's pyramid on selected nights. There were salacious tones of suspicious groans and mumbling, of lip smacking and heightened sighs – none of which were ever proven. What was proven was a tragic joke, how Henrietta attempted a visit to K's Egyptian relic found him stark naked on all fours, lowering a bent teaspoon into a well dug at the centre of the dirt floor, a teaspoon secured on a shoelace, from which he sipped water, one minute scoop at a time. The teaspoon story was much repeated, told with immediacy and authority by Henrietta's closest friends, which could mean there was an atom of truth or at least plausibility.

There were other untruths, made-up stories, speculations that K also survived on birds' eggs and wild fruit, on roots and berries, rumours quashed by Michael K's vegetable harvests, when nature yielded to his entombed wishes, his ownership of a portion of existence. There were evident and proven truths – if one could call them that – that K seemed to be a particle bouncing around in infinite space, a granule of obscurity and weightlessness. His harvest of vegetables was evidence, tangible proof, that Michael K, stripped of family and possessions, lived; his surest insurance against the future was his bucket of seedlings – dormant lives, plants destined to germinate. I wondered, if Michael would procure watermelons from our local supermarket, if Little Judas Groceries was not woefully stocked and deprived of fresh produce, would K have exchanged labour for wages, simplified the pains and anxieties inherent in farming? When plagued by unpredictable sleep patterns, what categories of sold labour would K have considered succumbing to: a scarecrow, a gravedigger, a consultant to bemused clients on the science behind pyramid architecture?

It must be that some people are conceived with hides for skin, with inbred defences against logic and palatable ideas, not because of any display of supernatural strength or convictions, but fragilities and vulnerabilities of pitiful leanings. Once or twice, hail damaged Michael K's pumpkin crops, prompting prolonged withdrawals into his pyramid. He was not sad, or hurt, not even indifferent, for there was a grain of distant concern in those vacant eyes, a realisation that something was amiss, diffused by immediate acceptance and unquestioning surrender to the imperfections of being.

There were times when I felt I irritated Michael K, particularly if I disturbed his sipping-water-from-a-teaspoon ritual. I found it bewildering that he couldn't simply scoop water using a mug or an old sardine can. Did quenching thirst have to be so torturous, so daunting, so complicated? Was it possible, I asked myself, that the teaspoon ritual had nothing to do with thirst but some form of otherworldly healing? Could it be that drinking water almost reduced to microscopic proportions signified grand gestures in the world of K, hazy with distortions and omissions? It was clear that his hearing was good, that his failure to respond to questions or participate in anecdotes was out of choice rather than some physiological limitation. Michael K was not a talker, which makes it impossible to decode whether the younger K spoke at all, if the boyish K took part in life, with all its demands and irritants. Not once did Michael K make me feel unwelcomed, though; it was because of my infrequent visits that I became aware that the pyramid dimensions were not concluded with visitors in mind; that for Mr K there seemed to be no distinction between fore-planning and plunging into chores, little regard for the impositions of time and common decency. Michael simply lived.

Numerous attempts, invitations and pleadings were extended to Michael K: by the local reverend, a Reverend Bell; by me in my official capacity as an unelected but nominated mayor (of sorts); by the Dust Island basket-weaving brigade, an assortment of peaceful delinquents concerned with basket weaving, not for sale but the good of Dust Island (baskets in varying shapes and sizes, to store grain, homemade bread; as secure little beds to rest toddlers in the shade; to hang from the rafters containing chicken eggs; as retreats for newly born and blind puppies).

And so, predictably, there remained many unknowns concerning Michael K: his views on government, on the fact that he might live never to witness or be trapped in another war. It was never clear whether he held any deep-set, personal, even dismissive opinions on the administration of wars – the one he had lived through or others that might erupt out of thin air. His general weariness and deceptive alertness made it impossible for anyone to solicit and secure even the most pedestrian commentary on anything, save for him nodding that it was a hot summer, or gently shaking his head when offered wood-roasted pork ribs. Had he always objected to feasting on dead animals, been committed to living off the soil? How was I to enter the inner workings of a heart whose owner seemed incapable of acknowledging grief (our funerals) or merriment (Dust Island's embarrassing but cherished weddings)? What did a kiss mean to Michael K, if anything? Had he been kissed before? Had a woman ever straddled him, lifted her dress to her navel, lowered herself onto his crotch, and guided his pulsating cock into her hallowed depths? What would such bliss have prompted him to do; to grin to himself while curling his toes to the wizardry of fucking and arousal, or would it have to him been an encroachment, an erosion of individuality?

An unseen, intangible force governs the landscape and light at Dust Island. A marked purity permeates the very form of the light, endowing it with luminous translucence, a crisp sharpness that seems to drain it of contaminants. This in turn gives Dust Island its picturesque beauty – the expansive plains, the distant blue-brown mountains, occasional heavy clouds that hang low, casting shadow patches across fallow ploughing fields. It is only when the Dust Island Devil comes, the spiteful easterly, that red dust is hoisted skywards, turning the scattered dwellings into an Island of Dust. The forces of heat, of dust and afternoon chills brew daunting storms, hailstones the size of infant palms, thus making life in Dust Island an eternal gamble. Only Michael K could solve the age-old problem – that of death by hailstones – by burying himself in an anthill until the worst of the storm had subsided. It was a mathematical solution, given that termite bites and the risk of a snake coiled in the anthill were lesser concerns than the flurry of frozen stones determined to fracture skulls. That was the Michael I knew. Resourceful. Patient. Adaptable.

I do not have the slightest doubt in my mind that Dust Island is heaven, a haven, for would-be poets – its brief tranquilities, its dust-storm turmoil, the elusiveness of its temperament. I have been planning to write poetry for years now, to soak my soul in feeling, drench my face with the compulsions of crystal moments, crucify myself on the altars of vanity and methodical debaucheries. But something always derailed me from my poetic passions, side-tracking me to the dreary worlds of the civil service. My directorship of Birth Registrations and the overseeing of asylum-seeker papers have no doubt blunted my poetic instincts, for my impromptu walkabouts in Johannesburg's hospital antenatal wards and refugee camps have exposed me to the furthest reaches of human depravities: newborns whose mothers were themselves orphans; drifters and immigrants arrested for modest and extreme violations of the immigration statutes; missing and fraudulent paperwork; expired permits and undeclared medical conditions; petty crimes and convoluted tales of strife and flight rendered in French and Portuguese, illuminated by hazy and desperate gestures. Speak

English, the arresting officers say. Are you Congolese or Mozambican? Your original home, your roots, you cannot be both. This here is not a genuine passport of the DRC – it's a suicide mission on your part. You think we're stupid? This one thinks we have time for games: lock him up! Such scenes drain the poetry wells within you; witnessing lost and desperate souls tell lies with such elaborate details – mostly made up – meant that it became impossible to appeal to my conscience. Africa belongs to all of us, exclaimed an elderly Moroccan herbalist in Jeppestown. We are one people; children of Mother Africa. No, it don't, interjected an arrogant trainee officer. This little piece of Mother Africa is called South Africa! Not Chad. Not Somalia. Not Malawi. We respect only genuine passports here – failing which you simply turn around and offer me your hands. Defective papers equal arrest. Simple mathematics. I wonder whether Michael K would have embraced such algebra, the mathematics of handcuffs, or if he was schooled in whatever ancient connections there were between the Shona and Luo, the Yoruba and Maasai. Did a voice crack through clouds, assail him while he hunkered down in caves, whisper to him what was to be expected of his future? Would that voice, its commands, have been the reason for K leaving Prince Albert, Sea Point, to come waste away in Dust Island? Or were there signs, small clues in his burrowing hole: broken snail shells, shiny crystals in the soil, twigs of a particular scent and diameter that demystified life into a coherent boon of prolonged sleep and pumpkin eating?

To be fair to him, Michael K did not strike me as a total recluse: he kept to himself, true, but life did not allow him to disappear entirely. In fact, some of our encounters were entirely of his design – or at the very least, his sensibilities. I remember him tracing on foot the contours of the perimeter fence, running his fingers along the wirework as if reconfiguring by touch the fence design; sitting cross-legged on an anthill as if in deep meditation; or squatting on the rim of a concrete dam (how did he, he of the jelly bones, manage to climb that dam unassisted?), listening to birdsong.

A word I associate with Michael K is presence; he was a very *present* being, in an absent kind of way. It is – and was – strange that such a detached being could project such power, that he, dreamy and unaffected, could reorder known worlds without uttering a single word. I must confess to having had – and continue to have – guarded admiration for him, acutely aware that I do not possess whatever it was that endowed his spirit with a distant glow, that sense of constant evolution, a measure of impenetrability.

At the same time, however, as much as I admired the man, I felt demeaned by that spiritual glow; how tacky its bolts, how rudimentary its hinges, how incomparable its design. I am disturbed by the thought that it is possible that I – with my PhD in Governance and Population Studies, with gowns and hoods meant to confirm my insights into Diplomatic Relations (Oxford University), part architect of a marriage that drowned in the flash floods of womanising and avid relations with Jack Daniels, the midwife of an astonishing spiritual reawakening, a saviour of the self – could be inferior to Michael K and his ilk. But, again, I have to concede that I have yet to encounter another specimen of his kind.

Unlike the thrills and magnetic buzz, the cosmopolitan daze and craze of Johannesburg, Dust Island seems light years away in its silence and almost tangible darkness. There is a great irony in that the quality of the light, sustained and transcendental, has to bow to the absolute darkness that blankets the landscape from earth to clouds and from horizon to horizon. There is primitiveness to the darkness, a veil, a completeness that haunts as much as it reassures: that light, in its varied strains and qualities, is impossible without the certainty of darkness. There is a terrifying beauty to the darkness – a nakedness of nature – how the power and majesty of lightning bolts chop through expansive horizons; how approaching storms can be heard sobbing and wailing and enraged from miles away; the audacious arrogance of thunderclaps echoing and reverberating to the furthest foot of the distant mountains. It seemed – and seems – to me that that whiff of sulphur, from tyrannical lightning blasting through space, contains the seeds of poetry, its breath, the very fibre of its nerve endings. Sobriety has brought with it a welcome range in thought and feeling, though I have not yet mastered that art of drinking water from a bent, looped teaspoon. How was it possible that tens, hundreds, maybe thousands of poets in Johannesburg committed their lives to verse and rhyme if none ever tasted, with their nostrils, the fading scent of discouraged clouds withdrawing rain, witnessed a mature rainbow hug whole mountain ranges, heard Michael K hum something hovering between melody and a worn-out dirge? How could their poetry be trusted, how could it be tumultuous and infecting, if they blunted their instincts, their senses, with supermarket food that bulged their bodies and dimmed their imagination? Wasn't there supposed to be sacredness demanded, commanded even, by poetry? Of what worth was poetry spray-painted on train station and morgue walls, where the penises of drunks and arsonists emptied bladders? How was such verse, burdened with the reek of urine, capable of purifying the soul, setting alight avenues of the mind? Or had I completely missed the point – mistook the effects of my Dust Island seclusion for insights, for enlightenment? Was it just loneliness creeping in, the reality of K's pyramid standing unoccupied, the stringed teaspoon still dipped in his well, in defiance of time and logic? Ideas and feelings in Dust Island are the closest to purity one can wish for in a lifetime, not so? So secluded and remote is our beloved little 'island' that technology has somehow turned a blind eye – no radio, no television, no newspapers – thus paving a way to an existential feast of heightened senses. But of what use were the nakedness of lightning bolts and the picturesque aerial cloud art if such inspiration leaked away, if such compulsions and tremors of the soul failed to yield a lone, impoverished, fledging line of poetry? How was I to know I had the markings of a poet if my memory and dreams battled scenes of refugee lines and faces of famished and despondent women: Russians, Tanzanians, Eritreans? How was it that K waltzed through life without ever having owned a passport? Was he never curious about the goings on in other faraway lands, the weather in other climes?

I have, since his passing less than a week ago, visited and inspected Michael K's pyramid in the hope of finding some clue, however meagre, with which to pry open his lizard tongue moistening cracked lips, lips that in life refused to divulge the stirrings of his soul. It soon dawned on me that this too was a futile effort, for what was to be deciphered from such sparse possessions? It was impossible to piece together any coherent sense of Michael K as a creature of ideas (what were they?), the sediment of human species. Unless one dabbled in artistic ponderings, it was and is daunting to know or establish a reliable interpretation of why anyone would think ownership of seedlings and a bent teaspoon, a burnt bucket, were enough to row through the murky waters of life and living. I found no obvious connections between K's pyramid and the Egyptian pharaohs (my knowledge of which is admittedly limited), or understood why K would drag relics of ancient civilisations into the present. Both Michael and his possessions remained a gesture of mythological proportions.

Had I failed in my attempt to unveil something, anything, of Michael from his cocoon? Would failure and disappointment continue to trail me? Wasn't it why I was here in the first place, to dissect and study the inner tubes of my being? Tucked away in the place, a part of me yearned for cosmopolitan living, for newspapers – itched to know what earth-shattering stories circulated across the Republic. I felt I had prematurely resigned myself from the noble and foolish acts of citizenship, from the dreary to the thrilling, the deceptive and catastrophic. None of these yearnings nudged me any closer to doing battle in the grand arenas of poetry – thus threatening my hard-won but brittle sobriety. Something alarms me, sneers at me that what I had convinced myself was recovery was a sham – for I still wake in the middle of the night craving Jack Daniels, my drink of choice, the one that had deceived me into succumbing to embarrassing excesses and stand-offs: me telling Eleanor Paine, my boss, to get off her fucking arse, go to the asylum safe houses, and see what immigration really *looks* like. She yelled (You are fired!) at the top of her voice in rage and disbelief, to which I calmly answered: Fired, my arse. Fuck you. You stink as a manager anyway. Everyone knows that but you. And that was that. Gross insubordination. Some grandstanding at my hearing. Dramatic tussles with old rivals and closet enemies, me stalking out, middle finger in the air, never to return.

An inherent tension, a contradiction of my being, is that I am a recovering drinker (not an alcoholic – there is a difference), essentially a disillusioned bureaucrat with artistic ambitions. These are complex matters to which to expose a mind, and I am not surprised that decades of attaching my signature to forms, to stamped letters and pleadings, paperwork to either advance or halt life-changing decisions, have lulled my sensibilities into thinking that shuffling state papers around is synonymous with living. Not so. It is the poetry I should have chased, kept hostage and owned.

But the world of verse has proven itself so elusive that I often asked myself what good would come of imposing upon a world a craft for which I possessed neither temperament nor talent. There would have been a small poem by now, some atrocious attempt, a six-liner perhaps, celebrating the magnificence of crimson moons, the luminance of celestial light, the tapestry of the Milky Way. I am still convinced that there might be an as-yet-undiscovered, overlooked path that will usher me into the furnaces of the poetic, where I will inhabit shadows of the greats, obliterate reputations of the hesitant, and live to be a hundred and fifteen with poetry oozing from my every pore, dripping from my every orifice.

I did not know Michael K to have been a religious man, which is not to say he was not a *spiritual* man. I had never had the opportunity to converse with him – if indeed it was conceivable to speak to Michael, his oppressively long pauses and head-nodding not consistent with conversations at hand – about the existence and obligations of God. I imagine it would have been a riveting exchange – or so cumbersome a chore that Michael would have elected to walk away, go bird-watching instead.

There are no famous deceased at the Twelve Apostles Cemetery – or at least that is what we thought until just over a week ago, when a familiar face appeared at Michael K's graveside. It must have been the only time that television and newspaper people descended on Dust Island, observing and recording the familiar face's minutest gestures. He was a man of average build, with bifocal lenses, denoting poor or unreliable eyesight. Not in the least talkative or conversational, it was hard to form any conclusive opinions as to why he had come, why he appeared so touched by Michael K's sudden but predictable death. The visitor was no doubt an accomplished man, followed around by Reuters and all manner of the world's news people, who insisted on and practically begged for 'just five minutes' of his time. I can't say the man was aloof; he certainly hinted at introvert tendencies, but smiled and nodded, acknowledged those who required his attention. He made it clear, however, by leaning closest to the ear of Reverend Bell, who was directing proceedings, that he preferred not to be singled out to say anything about the life and times of Michael K; he simply considered it a courtesy, common decency to pay his last respects to a man the news hordes proclaimed he knew intimately. There were no long speeches, mundane or famous, but emotive passages from Proverbs and Luke, as the Mohammed-designed coffin, reinforced with disassembled windmill blades, rested near a heap of red earth, with ropes ready to lift and lower it into the gaping hole. A reporter suggested he noticed a lone tear form in the famous visitor's left eye, but a counterview was that it could very well have been sweat. The scripture readings were poignant, the heat unbearable, the singing brief and functional, without notable courting of vocal and musical aesthetics. All the residents of Dust Island were in attendance, all thirty households, accompanied by Jerusalem the dog, who seemed curiously drawn to the singing. The famous man had arrived in a Land Cruiser, and dabbed his sweaty brow with a plain white handkerchief, until the hole had swallowed the coffin and a heap of earth confirmed that Michael K had acquired himself a grave. There are very few graves still, known through memory rather than elaborate inscriptions of headstones: Mohammeds to the east, Kubekas to the south, De Klerks southeast of the graveyard, while Mofokengs and Winterbottoms rested to the west. I introduced myself to the visitor as he nodded goodbyes through the open driver's window, the vehicle already creeping forward:

Miles. Ceremonial mayor of Dust Island. Closet poet.

He nodded, said, John.

I must have raised my brow, firing: Do you have a surname, John?

The news people had encircled the Land Cruiser by then, shoving feathery microphones through the car window, unleashing a disjointed symphony of camera shutters.

Yes, I do, answered the visitor.

Well?

Coetzee.

Wait a minute … John Coetzee? Nobel laureate?

That, too, yes.

How did you know the deceased?

I am going to miss my flight, he said.

Just briefly, please.

He sighed, said: I have known Michael since 1983, but in reality much earlier than that … I think it is sufficient to say we have come a long way.

How did you hear of his passing? interjected a stout woman who mentioned she owed her pay cheque to *The Irish Times*.

John Bailey, *BBC Radio 4*: Does his death bring closure for you, literary closure?

There is no closure in friendship or associations of whatever kind, answered John.

Susan Rice, *The Wall Street Journal*: Are there Colonel Jolls walking around Adelaide?

I am Jeffery Atkins from *The Daily Mirror*: The weight of fame must be cumbersome. How do you keep working, writing?

Frank Dube, SABC News: I loved most if not all of your work. But *The Master of Petersburg* is a terrible book – flat and tedious – or is my view misplaced?

The world is increasingly flooded with erotic, horror and pulp fiction. Do you think there is still a place for literary fiction in this century? asked Amina Adoo, of Al Jazeera.

Professor Brian Gikandi, University of the Western Cape: David Lurie is not exactly a remorseful beast, arrogant with what remains of a conscience. Did you intend of him to be so vile, such a contradictory man?

Mike Roberts; I am with the National Heritage Institute ...

Pauline Smith, *The Washington Post*: Not all Nobel laureates smell of roses, surely? Which in your view are – or were – painful creatures to encounter, that is, underserving daughters and sons of bitches? Laughter.

The Ethiopian Times, Cinda Kawenda: Do you feel the manner of this death will alter your mode of writing, what critics have already written and concluded?

But how did you hear of the passing? repeated Elizabeth Glasgow, *The Irish Times*.

John half raised the car window, engaged Drive, released the handbrake and let the Land Cruiser roll forward. He gazed ahead, reflectively ... Telepathic connection, he said, and drove off.

Professor Gikandi, who seemed to me an intelligent man, curious and alert, asked whether I had known Michael K well. I answered that that was relative, for I was not convinced it was possible for anyone to really know K. He was not a knowable man. It was fair to say I associated with him, but ambitious to claim I knew him well enough to commit to such a conclusion. Gikandi's whole premise for asking the question was that people did not attend funerals of complete strangers for no reason – that it would make no sense that I stood in the blazing sun if there were no compelling reasons for closure, for memories, for a send-off. He, Professor Gikandi, could not contain his 'utter exhilaration' that he had stood shoulder to shoulder with a Nobel laureate at a cemetery (not the most ideal or enchanting of places, admittedly), though he lamented that fame often blinded the less famous when in the sudden and unexpected company of the famous, prompting the less famous into awkward and thoughtless speech, hasty and uninformed conclusions, speculative yearnings.

It could not be said, opined the professor, that either of us has truly met the Nobel laureate, that it was impossible to claim we had, for the blinding light fame imposes on people. That we could not, in reality, conclude that we understood what he meant by 'telepathic connection'; that even if we did understand, we could not in all fairness expect to unpack a telepathic whatever that started before 1983 into neat and universally accepted understanding. That because of fame the less famous had always, since time immemorial, nodded away daunting misunderstandings for fear of not paying due attention to greatness, for failing to distinguish between rea_

people and their life of fame. Fame, said the professor, made it impossible to be truly honest and insightful – the reason he found Frank Dube's statement to the Nobel laureate (that *The Master of Petersburg* was an atrocious book) not only courageous but brave. Because fame demands certain standards of being, of restraint, it was daunting even for the famous to master the art of restraint, a failure often and wrongly dismissed as arrogance. The luminance of good fame, not infamy, pondered the professor, was dependent on partial abandonment of the self in recognition and worship of that fame. Worship, however brief or detached. It was difficult, he said, to separate cancers from good cells – to, like a surgeon, direct a scalpel into moments of time, into the lives of famous and even average people, into the secret passions of artists, to determine and savour the finest veins that separate fact from fiction. Famed writers, mused the professor, weave art and fame and real life so seamlessly that it is expected of them to be otherworldly and out of reach, for characters they create to mirror their deepest visions, reflect their entombed passions. I must admit that what the professor said sounded intelligent, but I could not understand what fame had to do with a dead recluse, how Michael K fitted in in the talk about us not having truly met John Coetzee. How could that be when the man was standing right next to me – when I could see the sweat on his brow and the red dust on his shoes? Literature is a world on its own, concluded the professor, and unless immersed in its expansive lakes, it is impossible for a former bureaucrat to understand – which is radically different from appreciating the enigma that is literary compulsions. Big English, I said to him, prompting him to grin with satisfaction.

There must have been more to Michael K than just the phantom, the recluse, the vagabond. There must, surely, have been something great that Michael K was or should be famous for – or, if not famous for, that he could have taught humanity without resorting to pitiful withdrawals and starvations? I could not pin down one thing that would justify the status of sage being awarded to K, but I found it impossible simply to dismiss him as a worthless fool. There was something there – a distant knowing that lit his eyes, perhaps a swarm of thoughts he had no vocabulary or interest to express. But that could not possibly be true, for the world is full of vagabonds of all hues, none of whom aspire to the same tortures. Every recluse somehow retains some level, however small, of a personal imprint on his awkwardness. Michael K was perhaps the most extreme, but not necessarily the rarest. There should, I thought to myself, be Ks sleeping under bridges or journeying vast open plains: in New Zealand or Antananarivo? What made *this* K special, interesting enough to command the attention of Nobel laureates? Was it unthinkable that such esteemed individuals would think a specimen such as Michael a nuisance, or was delving under the skins of misfits (historical, societal, cultural) the very ingredients necessary to impress the Nobel committee – precisely because it should be draining and demanding piecing together lives of Ks of this world, who exist beyond laws and time?

I suppose one can attribute K's demise to 'natural causes' – though that in itself says very little, as it does not, in the absence of pathology reports, pinpoint with any measure of exactitude what would have triggered the ultimate and final snapping of the twine that secures the soul to bosoms. It is not an immaterial paradox this, for cause of death is a significant colourant of the intensity and duration of mourning or grief, so much so that science has been perfected over the years to reveal in photographic, diagrammatic and narrative details the final nail in the coffin – pun completely intended. What Michael's life proves, judging from its exterior markers, is that a life of strife is not fatal in and of itself, just as indifference and idealism (planned, circumstantial or accidental) provide no elixirs against the hooks of mortality. Death seems to me the only true democracy – a democracy that has perfected elongation of its claws and tentacles to the furthest reach of human habitats. Michael simply failed to appear, two mornings in a row, prompting me to investigate. (Truth is I wanted to find out whether he had any sunflower seeds to spare, but that is neither here nor there.) And so I found him. Arms neatly folded on his chest, a hint of a smirk on his face, personal belongings (the teaspoon, the bucket with seedlings, the gardening tool a remnant of the Iron Age) by his side, his departure was evidently free of haste and not sudden. It might seem strange, but it is a fact that I am – surprisingly, but not inconceivably – in mourning. A gaping hole has been excavated at the epicentre of my being. Such a total loss that I often wake in a cold sweat, shocked and bewildered. Michael was my friend – a friend in the furthest sense of the word. I cannot commit to stories and anecdotes, to elaborate memories and mutual plans, for our friendship cannot be said to have been of the conventional kind. It was marked by a mute connection of thoughts, by long, drawn-out and palpable silences. There was a fondness there, a flickering glow, beautiful and fragile, but *present* nevertheless.

When I think about it now, it seems to me that the Nobel laureate did not hear me when I mentioned I was a closet poet, or maybe he was too distracted by the news people descending on the Land Cruiser like a swarm of bees.

It can be said that, in a way, Poet Hendricks was himself a closet poet for committing poetry to tree trunks and out of reach, out of view in caves. Nature offered no guarantees that such poetic toils would endure, that they would be protected (heavy rains, veld fires, lightning strikes), that anyone would understand what was written, or equate it to a flesh-and-blood person, a poet. Did poets do that, raise their hands to proclaim themselves poets, without being asked? What was John expected to say, to do?

Pedro Rigarro is a kind man, by which I mean I do not know his unkind and agitated side, whom I have never seen enraged or deceitful, or been in his company when he was being cruel and domineering, or pompous and insulting. A Mozambican national, he sells his time, portions of his life, to Peninsula Trucking Inc. and drives a truck with Cape Town plates to Dust Island the last Monday of every month. His trips here seem futile, but the truth is we would be completely divorced from civilisation if his truck voyages ever came to an end. He brings basic groceries to the Little Judas supermarket (and collects woven baskets to be sold in the city), and the twenty-litre paraffin ration to illuminate Dust Island homes. Twenty divided by thirty is one and a half litres of paraffin per household per month – the arithmetic of liquids, intended for Dust Island lanterns.

According to Pedro, who is neat by nature and tackily dressed by circumstance, he found Michael K fast asleep on the yellow line of the R572 and had, as Pedro's truck approached, perhaps dreaming, rolled further into the road into the way of the speeding truck. Michael K's foetal position on the tarmac made him look like a tortoise, and it was only on closer observation that Pedro realised it was a human being fast asleep on the tar. No, he wasn't drunk; neither was he suicidal or insane. Having had dew descend on him during his overnight walk, his body simply craved the warmth offered by the tar. A thawing ritual. Asked about his intended destination, Michael K had told Pedro that he had no particular place in mind; all he required was a remote and secluded place, preferably with good soil, where he could engage in a little farming. Where was he from, laden with a bucket and a self-made gardening tool? Sea Point, he had answered. K did not necessarily need a ride in Pedro's truck, but didn't mind if such an offer was made. He did not seem in the least perturbed that sleeping on public roads was not only deadly but illegal, and welcomed the opportunity to doze off and snore his way to wherever the truck would take him.

When Pedro pulled up outside Little Judas in Dust Island, he had asked K what he thought of the place and, waking from deep slumber, K had narrowed his eyes, tugged at his overgrown beard and said: I have seen better places, but this will do for now. That is how Michael K came to Dust Island – mistaken for a tortoise, and almost run over by Pedro's truck.

The last many evenings have been restless and filled with angst. That Dust Island is harsh on us all is true, but I am further strangled by bouts of insomnia I have never known – the dim lantern light attracting nocturnal insects, the pen present and impotent in my hand. Poetry won't come, not even small badly drawn cartoon characters or plant leaves, not even variations of my name in different handwriting styles. And yet my signature had come so easy unfelt, devoid of consciousness, when I set in motion instructions and approvals to refer matters for deportations, conditional extensions for continued stays on humanitarian grounds. It was corrosive having to remind myself that papers before me were mirrors, blooming flowers or swords given to breathing humans of flesh and blood. But slowly, over time, I began to reach for the Jack Daniels every time I felt suspicious of or burdened by my power, a power conferred on me by the state with the assurance that I would act as both custodian and night watchman to ensure as many *known* Zimbabweans or Ugandan persons worked in the banking corporates or sewage plants of Johannesburg. I became increasingly disconnected from the power I was purported to have, to wield, and I sobbed on heaps and hillocks of official papers, paralysed by my failure to attach a signature. Corridor murmurs grew to heated exchanges – for my subordinates were too careful and unsure how to confront me and I, on the other hand, had not worked out the wording appropriate and weighty enough to give voice to my gradual reservations with the almost Godlike powers entrusted in me: powers to decide on the movement and freedom of other sickly, destitute, traumatised, fleeing, despairing, stateless, famished, skilled, useful, noble and wise human beings, and other countless categories, including beautiful and kind-hearted.

When you are as young as I was, twenty-six, the limits of power seem remote and unknown. Insignificant. Work at that tender age adds headaches and hours; pay progressions dull the mind into equating power to reality – to it being owned and timeless when, in reality, power has been wielded and enshrined and suspected and abused for centuries, until it withers into nothingness.

I realised at forty-nine that the same power entrusted in and wielded by Ramses or Churchill, authority by birthright (very suspicious) or borrowed, thrived on the refusal to answer questions. I knew that terrain well – avoiding the intrusion and nuisance of questions: what happened, where and why. I rose several ranks having mastered the nuances of authority – but not its pitfalls. Warm-blooded humans became statistics in my reports: 26, 36, 18.6 per cent; they became graphs, faceless and stateless hordes, who no doubt cursed or prayed for the Good Lord to guide my mighty pen, a few strokes of which could secure sound sleep or bruising calamities. Such power robbed the conscience of shade, exposing it to harmful rays. One got used to presiding over lives, to being listened to, expected to sign internal memoranda laced with heartlessness. I increasingly found myself staring at my office walls past midnight, immobilised, asking: to whom does Africa truly belong? Did I *truly* possess powers to determine the movement and whereabouts of those who belonged to it, who were from and of it?

Events and scenes in office 603 on the fourteenth floor of the State Security Complex harmed my natural disposition to humour and light-hearted musings, and thus slowly deformed me into this grim tyrant with easy tears and Jack Daniels breath. I find it painfully amusing that the state had been so generous with the powers entrusted to me, powers with which I could order men to oversee heart-warming and harrowing things, that I could, with the stroke of a pen or ear on the telephone receiver, express my gratitude or dismay to heads of embassies far and wide: congratulatory courtesy calls or tense letters denouncing unsavoury events or dubious characters. How little that power has turned out to be, how deprived of human worth its tentacles, casting obscene shadows on the conscience.

My brief hospital stay (alcohol poisoning) seems to many to have been triggered by my father placing the Smith & Wesson in my hand, when it was, in fact, also a slow erosion of all the inner bridges that gave my soul its colour, my thoughts their cooling breeze, and my womanising its shamelessness. I understood and empathised with Father's desperation, how doctors had notified him of a medical necessity to gouge his eyeballs out in order to prevent the cancer from spreading to the brain. He lamented prospects of life without vision, and bewildered and alone decided that a bullet was not an unheard-of release, except that he lacked the courage to see it through.

I suddenly miss home, am besieged by a taste of gall that threatens to snuff my breath, frustrated by the thirty-one months of my life wasted in Dust Island, waiting for poetry. Pedro says it will cost a hundred rand to hitch a ride into Cape Town, that he could if I am lucky choose airport routes on his way back to Peninsula Trucking Inc. What have I done to myself, trapped in this outpost where living means gritting teeth, where the rest of the world seems not to exist? I will tiptoe to Amu's house, knock lightly and thrice at her window at minutes past midnight, kiss her on the forehead, rub her long back with open palms, squeeze her hips fleetingly, then kiss her open and delirious mouth, and announce in a whisper:

I am here.

I know you are. What do you want?

You.

I see. And I am the most beautiful woman under the stars, right?

Dead right. Tallish, with diamond earrings, a chipped tooth and radiant smile, yes, with a hint of a dimple on the left cheek, she is delightful. An inspiring pair of baby-feeding and lover-scorching breasts, weighing ten grams each, speculatively, give or take. And

37

that chest button left open? That is never a mistake. Women are very particular about their dress: how the skirt sits on the hips, no panty lines, the correct bra fit, in the right colour and not at odds with the blouse, comfortable stilettos. Twinkle in her eyes. Good brain. Firm personality. No pushover. Not a slouch in bed, either. You only have to see the curvature of her back for that, the steady hips, engineered for a lifetime of surprises. She is a beautiful woman, too beautiful, maybe. Those wrists. Subtle. Sculptured. Perfect.

You want me right now?

I wanted you one, seven, eleven days ago.

Come then, my Shakespeare. Bring your puppy eyes and flaming self hither. And ... lock the door. Isn't it terribly bad mannered doing things with your landlady?

In centuries past, maybe. Not any more.

Your rent is a week late.

I know. It shall be paid a thousand times over, in currency and a flaming heart.

You still haven't changed your mind? What is there in Johannes-burg that you cannot find here?

Intensity. Madness. Jazz.

And me?

I will come visit.

Do you truly love me, or do you just crave my biscuit?

I adore you. Your biscuit can answer for itself.

There will be an avalanche of kisses. Buttock grabbing. Spiritual flight.

JOHANNESBURG, AGAIN

Johannesburg skies can, when it rains, seem either like waterfalls or avalanches have been let loose, or drizzle in misty gentle showers that sharpen the senses. It is as though one can count individual raindrops gliding past the balcony lights and commit mass suicide on the paving. It is on evenings such as this that I listen to the music of the rain – its windy intervals, diminished hail splattering on the patio tiles, the music of heavenly ice splintering into general rain cold and indistinguishable.

I have, like a sacrificial lamb, returned to Johannesburg to dare fate, surrender the perks of peaceful living to the more fortunate. I have become faceless, jobless – no more a bureaucrat. Professor Von Ludwig has complicated what I thought would be my next life. It is doubtful I will ever be a poet, though I continue to see the beauty and the rot in things. I am an undecided patriot maybe, suspicious of some cynical bandits for countrymen who wipe their anuses with the country's flag, who use it to cover vomit and corpses of well-meaning and upright countrymen. There cannot be poetry in that – not even its slightest shadow. Or maybe poetry is not seen with the naked eye; maybe sight is an inferior tool with which to capture poetry; maybe poetry is more a felt thing than a thought one. But if Von Ludwig is right, how possible is it to feel anything if one cannot think it through? Wasn't the mind, thought, according to Von Ludwig, the stream from which all human passions and depravities drink?

I, following the collapse of a nine-year marriage, took transfer of a two-bedroom apartment from Blue Eagle Estates, a secluded little piece of earth at Moon Dust 6, a lavish haven of modern townhouses that scream cosmopolitan snobbery. I live alone. Maureen comes on Wednesdays and Fridays and she, when the laundry is folded and, on occasions, the cooking is done, says: I will see you next Wednesday, sir. I smile at her, nod. I sometimes drive her to the taxis – endure fragmented small talk: that she does not like politicians, is allergic to fish, and cannot stand Gregorian chants. I tell her about the dust storms of Dust Island, and we muse about what needs to be done to ease peak-hour traffic. In truth, I am glad that Midrand's vehicular life is barely crawling. Maureen is young, extremely private and, for man sluts without principles, a worthy companion in matters of love and lust. She is, strictly speaking, too young for such entanglements. One has to be a real brute to act on such compulsions, so I call her 'Daughter' or 'Baby Girl' as insurance, a potential instinct that has to extinguish fiery loins on unexpected occasions; remember that the poor thing belongs to her age mates (or maybe she belongs only to *herself!*), young and inexperienced men and would-be women; that she deserves some grain if not a whole measure of her purity in Johannesburg's grand love theatres – where the comedy and tragedy of young innocents succumb to the brutalities of cosmopolitan savagery. There is, as the traffic crawls, as the rain pours down with mindless beauty, a magnetic buzz that fills my Volvo, stolen glances I allow myself when Maureen looks out the window: her beautiful ears, the erotic charge sparked by the seatbelt holding portions of her breasts in temporary captivity, and those charming, beguiling and sculpted legs concealed in dark navy Levis. I ask her to read for me sometimes, a poem an hour whenever she rests between chores. Or I let her watch television. Surprisingly, *WWF Raw* and perhaps predictably, reruns of *Keeping Up with the Kardashians* and *The Fashion Police*. She has hazy and sometimes apprehensive views on what becomes of Zoology majors, to which I joke: Don't they immunise monkeys against tuberculosis or explain the birthing distress of elephants? She smiles: teary eyes, a knowing but respectful mouth (has she ever been kissed?) and the posture of a banking CEO. She is pretty, calm-spirited, though her personality seems to me to not be yet fully formed, a gift to be admired and protected. Our conversations are brief and sanitised: I tell her about Dust Island, but not the dirty dreams she provokes in me. I cannot show her Father's Smith & Wesson, or share the full story behind that illegal inheritance. No words of my nocturnal combats with poetry ever leak from me, to say nothing of the late realisation of how unsuited for matrimonial confinements I am, how – even without the Jack Daniels – the lipsticks, intruding earrings, the odd suspicious phone call from one of my lonely or agitated lovers, I do not possess in me the average heat to sustain roasting withdrawals and petty skirmishes: arguments over toothpaste lids, an accidental urine droplet on the toilet seat and, of course, the Jack Daniels transgressions. I, to counter the gloominess, sometimes request Maureen to read me Isaac Hayes and Dolly Parton lyrics from the back of my LPs, music that comforts and bewilders, in the hope of a poetic line. It never comes.

Instead, I caution and remind myself that I am an ageing man with responsibilities that preclude me from chasing carefree thrills. I drive Maureen (a forbidden fruit, she is not the kind of love to be sampled with a teaspoon, not even a tablespoon, because what it needed was not only *quantity* but also *immediacy*: it needed to, like urgent pain medication, be gobbled intravenously) to the taxis, and return home to poignant and sometimes hollow efforts of The Temptations or Commodores. How naked the words become without their famed melodies and musical accompaniment, how wise and futile the knowledge of human sorrow and yearning woven into art, how timeless and static the world of each song, how varied and deceptive the private voyages that birth and anoint songs into poetry of an elastic time period, a culture.

Seven weeks pass. Maureen is on the phone, on the balcony, sitting lazily and carefree on the cane furniture sipping coffee and painting her toes a deep red. It is her lunch hour, you see. Brenton, she says to a friend whose name is Mildred, is a good old man. Four thousand rand he gave me, and the biggest flower bouquet I have ever seen. His tongue-fucking skills are not too shabby for an oldish man, and he can be a demon in bed when he wants. Yes, sometimes ... well, that depends. Really? I told you *that* already? Shocking! I tell you far too much, and will have to kill you if you decide to no longer be my friend. No. He is not controlling in any way. No, it's not that at all. He's a busy man – always out of the country to all these faraway places. Berlin. Spain. Wales. He brings me gifts – tons of gifts. And as you already know, he is super cute.

I choke on an ice cube, stand transfixed, my eyes tearing from unexpected suffocation and a sudden heartache. I shuffle away, tiptoe upstairs, to calm a raging heart and ease a brutalised throat. I think: the things we hold dear, sacred. How vile and deceptive the mute bells of innocence whose sudden din blinds and lacerates. Am I in love with her, without knowing it? Is it possible that a heart can be defiant, so sneaky, that it decides on its own to leap from mountain peaks, of love and the unknown, without the owner's consent? What, if she has a globetrotting old man, is Maureen doing working for me, a comatose would-be poet with a fast-diminishing pension fund?

Of course I worry about money; I worry about money all the time. I am without a plan or will have to wake at six in the morning to impose questionable powers on other human beings: refugees and asylum seekers. It is strange how worthless my signature has become – it can no longer consent to the immediate arrest or release of a wrongfully arrested Shona orphan with a hip fracture, cannot decide who is granted immunity or pardon against errors of judgement, cannot even in a roundabout way cast the ultimate deciding vote for improved quality of toilet paper for the office. Kind consideration for people's arses but not for children in the clutches of fever in holding cells in some Johannesburg corner or other.

My restraint, my visions of Maureen's innocence have been dealt a death blow, shattered into a million pieces by the not-so-young Brenton who drives a gull-wing Mercedes, a noisy and imposing little thing, who comes to pick Maureen up on selected days. He is self-aware, reserved, fully conscious that plundering Maureen's youth has its gains and silent judgements. He hides his eyes behind Burberry sunglasses, never disembarks from the Mercedes and always waves from afar.

When Maureen started declining my offers to drive her to the taxi rank, the sudden shock lent to the heart a tinge of sadness. She has purity about her, a grace, a bewitching charm that radiates pleasure and promise. It is easy to forget she is still, all things considered, realistically but not technically speaking, not a mature woman. She, in my estimations, still needs to fool around with a boy or two, find her feet, and not plunge herself into worlds of old men and their appetites, their distorted lives. But who knows? Maybe earth-shattering wisdom is imparted between his tongue fucking.

Johannesburg is Johannesburg. It is not Dust Island. Was it possible, I asked myself, that a single city, the sprawling metropolis that is Johannesburg, could have a life of its own – not the life of people who inhabit it, but how those people give it its lifeless life in concrete and electrical wires, in lit bridges and emblazoned billboards advertising BMWs and Rolex watches, gridlocked traffic and billowing cloud, a life heavy with history and fragments of greatness, all its miraculous achievements and false starts seeping through the city's defective pores?

There is no place on earth that remotely apes its Johannesburgness: the urgent, thrilling, addictive pull that has captivated, nurtured and amputated varied souls over time. I know the city too well maybe, for I have been in and out of its many buildings, its homes and graveyards – as a friend, a worker, a lover and discreet hound for its artistic life: the Goodman Gallery on Jan Smuts Avenue, the theatrical births at the Market Theatre, jazz sips and spillages at the Wits Great Hall or the Teatro at the Montecasino, Africa Day plumes and ornaments, Salif Keita piercing the evening breeze with a voice both noble and supreme, as haunting as it is embalming.

I look for poetry in every crevice of the city, scrape the City Hall bannisters in the hope of collecting poetry residue left by visiting and hosted poets: poetry preservation by the fingernail. I stand transfixed at the City Hall staircases, head tilted back, mesmerised by the beauty and symmetry of chandeliers that rain light droplets and avalanches onto the foyer, with its vacuumed carpeting and officialdoms. I sniff for verse by touch on the lift buttons, pressed by millions of fingers over time – dignitaries, artisans, assassins, newspaper people, priests and fraudsters, the fingers and thumbs of prostitutes and of idealists, the knuckles of politicians and elbows of despondent clerks, messengers of the Sheriff, obese children of Johannesburg's socialites, pickpockets alongside pizza-delivery boys and florists scrutinising delivery address slips, clean-shaven candidate attorneys jostling for lift space alongside morose lifetime cleaners chewing gum and the odd puppy or parrot permitted to enter the hallowed spaces and high ceilings of City Hall, its pillars and period sneers.

I slide my moccasins on the floor of the elevator, attempt to detect the smallest granule of sand buried in the carpeting. The faintest connection between atoms, how that single granule has been crushed by millions of shoes, carved and resized, chiselled into a particle of existence embedded in the green-and-gold tufts, a granule whose true origins could have been the construction sites of Abu Dhabi, for it is impossible to tell the origins and movement of sand granules. Was K that, a sand granule, blown about by earthly winds because of his worthlessness and near weightlessness –

existing to be crushed and corroded and discarded, left to the obscurity of elevator floors?

I suspect that my greatest downfall is the discovery of my God-given passion: a compulsive and obsessive fascination with all things literature, the life of art, as opposed to confusing working for the state with a life calling. How absurd it now seems that stamping refugee and asylum-seeker papers could ever constitute a whole life, that such a life would be charmed and worthwhile. The discovery of my second heart – the artistic hammer that pounded at my ribcage for days on end – completely altered how I saw the world, how I embraced negligible but potent secrets life had held from me for decades. My desire for a heightened life, a life of passion and of creation, a life that would outlive me by thousands of years, a life of a famous poet, was almost dealt a death blow by a man I love to hate, one who says in one of his writings: art too is just a way of living. Yet my disappointment remains guarded and unsure, for I do not understand enough about literature or the full works of Rilke to be forceful in my objection, to understand the basis of this seemingly reckless statement, which stands in direct contrast with the lucidity of his thoughts, the fire in his verse.

My solace is music; it has always been – so much so that I have cultivated it to ritualistic heights in the manner and frequency of my listening sessions. I consider myself a purist with little patience for techno and mindless pop. I am and remain a Bob Dylan hound, a Nina Simone disciple, a student of Sixto Rodriguez. At Miles Davis's feet I have cobbled my wings, wings that continue to allow me momentary flight every time 'Time After Time' plays, every time Miles removes the mute from his trumpet, puts aside its vulnerable sound, embalms the soul with the rich and rounded trumpet sermons on 'New Blues', a sensory musical feast that, in its beauty, tickles the finest hair tips and rattles root canals of teeth. Salif Keita is of course never far – how I plunge into his vocal ballads and chants, his impassioned laments, the edginess of his celebratory yearnings; how I (on television) follow him across the stages of Paris and all of America, of Johannesburg and Amsterdam, mesmerised. I contend and ask: when will my poetic spark ignite?

I wonder, Jack Daniels in hand, whether Michael K had any musical tastes or preferences, if he could distinguish between 'I Shot the Sheriff' and 'Amazing Grace', if he ever had the inclination to muse at an arresting lyric, to have his heart flutter and lift at the devilish eloquence of Lionel Richie's 'Three Times A Lady'.

There were evenings, humid and without spiritual harmony, when I thought about Michael K and his brief time at the Cape Rail Company, when Lightnin' Hopkins and BB King and Eric Clapton so saddened me with the blues that I couldn't help but let out a muted tortured cry, brief and self-conscious, like a lost puppy suddenly realising eminent danger. My thirst for the poetic seemed to double every time I was alone, and it soon became feverish and pathological, such that I could not sleep or eat or exist without seeing life as little beauty fragments (Michael K's toes, the furious grace with which Nina Simone massages or pounds piano keys, Maureen's habit of stirring her coffee anticlockwise) and the uncertain ugliness of unformed poetic instincts.

It dawned on me at thirty-seven or thereabouts that it was possible that I had thrown away decades of my life as a hesitant bureaucrat – that a second heart was forming and foaming alongside my known and dreary life, that my true calling was never to have been trapped in the dim lights of state affairs and protocols, but to soar towards the immeasurable horizons of art and feeling.

The true beauty of my life, thus far, is perhaps the fact that I have always endeavoured to live it with unguarded passion. I might have overestimated my worth in the universe, though. But that cannot be a crime, surely, for those who know me will attest that I have never intentionally been an egotistical man. Mine was a simple and humble error in existential arithmetic – thinking the number was *ten* when it was in fact *three*. I decided, after three days of meditation – not always as immersive as I had hoped – to plunge myself into the orbit of studies. My every artistic limitation, it seemed to me, stemmed from the nagging discomfort that I was simply uninformed as to the workings and perils of literature – that as hard as I tried there remained dim avenues that remained out of reach, that demanded a cultivated knowledge that I simply did not have.

I got lost on my way to the African Literature department, and had the misfortune and obscure blessing of being directed thence by a Von Ludwig: Head, Wits Department of Philosophy. The professor does not have ramp-model looks, but has, as he points out, a Von Ludwig mind, with piercing but knowledgeable eyes that have captivated lecture halls for decades. He has chosen to reject the indignities of a wig, wears his balding head with the brazen defiance of a man confident of his achievements. His dress sense (three-piece suits) is commanding without being flamboyant, that of a public intellectual in the age of television and glossy magazines. Manicured nails, moist lips that pronounce words with vigour and precision, the neatest of moustaches betray countless hours of scholarly slavery, confirmed only by bloodshot eyes and a verbal confession: I have been an owl for weeks, sir. In the precarious trenches of grading examination scripts. To decide whether frail and shaky arguments on morality and fate by well-meaning and often hardworking students constitute philosophy.

Aren't you a bit advanced in age to fancy sharing lecture halls with brats?

No, I am not. This is something I have to do.

Have to do or want to do?

Have to do.

Von Ludwig chuckles: I see.

That sets off so many questions. It is going to take us a hundred years to sift through them all.

Anyway, he says, we are not a bad department ourselves, in crafting and polishing minds. Thinking is the basis of everything, is it not? I wouldn't go as far as to dismiss literature as inferior, but I am convinced, with years of practice of course, that philosophy is to the mind what rain is to life. What would be the point of being presented with basic or complex problems of life and living if one is incapable of thinking, of seeing all sides to a thought, possessing the capability of magnifying its minutest deceptions? Soyinka, Hamsun, Marías, Kafka – worthless without a properly cultivated mind. Well, maybe not as extreme as that, but you get the picture. Even daredevils employ the safety of parachutes, sir. Maybe I am just a lost and disillusioned cynic, but I cannot see life without a mind bolted down by range and plurality of thought. Even thoughts about thoughts. Why study stories – for that is what literature essentially is – without a mind fully equipped to dissect them? I have application forms on my desk. What do you say?

I feel pressured: I'll think about it, Professor Von Ludwig.

Plus, he interjects, I have family and associates who have known Rilke and Goethe in person. Not some fuzzy, distant biographies commissioned for commercial reasons. I mean people who hosted and shat in the same toilets as Søren. Even Sartre. Shared cigarettes with him. I have an uncle, Marko, who has original postcards from Camus when he was sickly and despondent, battling tuberculosis in the Alps. My godmother, Helena Hess, God bless her wretched soul, taught German philosophy until her teeth fell out at the miraculous age of a hundred and eleven. Which is not to say she was any good – quite the contrary – but I have to admit that her passion was admirable and exemplary. You will hear a lot of reckless talk about philosophy being dead and some philosophers outdated, to be admired from a distance, but that is all worthless talk from poseurs and mental invalids. I have a class of seventeen – the sharpest minds around, scalpel- and laser-like – and missing the eighteenth mind to complete us. Your mind will thank you for it.

I admire your passion. Thank you. But I still have to think about it.

That is what philosophers do, my good sir. Think. But with a goal in mind. How beautiful and enigmatic the elusiveness and grandeur, the discovery and purity of thoughts, sir. Do sleep on it, with the full and assured comfort that you have a key into the German philosophy and literary history in yours truly, Professor Von Ludwig, shepherd of cerebral flocks uprooted from Baden-Württemberg and implanted in Johannesburg since 1985.

There is no doubt that he is ageing gracefully, those ocean-blue eyes still full of spark and thoughtful glimmers, of average height and banker attire, Henry Kissinger glasses. It is late afternoon, late December, the academic year having been depleted, save for student enquiries or therapeutic meetings and grievances over unremarkable grades. The hallways echo footsteps and voices in motion, drills and hammers as handymen go about their business. Philosophy professors were either locked in their offices, on sabbatical or deceased, except this Von Ludwig man with the curly hair characteristic of music composers and designers.

Literature is not what it used to be, he says. It is a grave but not punishable mistake to assume that all poetry is the same, that poetry in whatever language serves the same purpose. Sure, there are rules of grammar, sir – or rather rules of poetic practice – but like music or the visual arts, the sheer scale of poetic invention is so great as to overwhelm any rational thought. That said, there is poetry that appeals to love or fluffy feelings of giddiness, sentiments of yearning and admiration committed to paper, and there are poems written in blood: those of war and revolution. We don't have the time to examine all known or possible categories, suffice to say that it is not enough to aspire to be a poet without having resolved some basic pains that ultimately claw the poetry out of you. Not all poets bleed, sir – and until such time that poetry becomes a matter of life and death, creation so potent that it snuffs the breath out of your lungs, momentarily stops your heart, you cannot be cloaked in the robes of a poet. I come from a family of poets – famous ones, important ones, obscure ones, poets who have written and taught poetry for decades. So I have it on good authority that poetry is not the essence of life but its element. Let me pose a question if you squeeze juice (poetry) from an orange (life), is the juice the same as the orange? Tricky proposition, but also a worthless inquiry The most famous of the poets from the Ludwig family tree, Hans von Ludwig – a poetry deity in Munich and Stuttgart and Berlin a much more accomplished music composer than he was a poet – is most famous for dying in the hands of a prostitute than any of the famous poems that are to this day the very fabric of German culture. Literary historians have yet to establish and probe that he my uncle Hans, is related to Franz Kappus by intricate and debatable ancestries through intermarriage, which you would, if you were tuned into the world of literature, know is no more than a drop in research standards. The truth is that art can be very murky, sir. A greater truth is that poetry requires both ruthlessness and sensitivity in equal measure: creation from contradictions. That is before the weight of fame sets in, for fame soon becomes a struggle to keep the natural order and innocence of things. You understand?

I smile, nod. He continues.

There is a lot of artistic aping going around, a poverty of original ideas. Why would you want to spend what remains of your years in a declining field – which is not to say, of course, that it would be completely worthless, without prospects of renewal, but why? Philosophy, on the other hand, is the cornerstone of reflection and invention, of throwing thoughts into the stratosphere. Doesn't that sound like a charming place to be? Come now, my scholar. Give it a try. You can always change to your original love – literature – if you think philosophical passions mundane. Even then, having decided that philosophy is a dreadful bore, you can always come for coffee, to office 137, that one with a silly poster of a man sticking out his tongue. Einstein. A man of German leanings.

On the other hand, says Professor Von Ludwig, it is worth affirming that the residue of an age, of a whole civilisation, its afflictions, resides in the fierceness of its art, its poetry. It is from the poets that we search for fragments of lives lived, of history away from historians, of emotions imprisoned in ink: the battalions of flies that rose from corpses in Auschwitz, the perfect imperfect symmetry of the maple leaf, and ruins of people and things that were never strong or interesting or sacred enough to endure the tyrannies of time.

He stops.

Oops – it's already four o'clock. I'd better get going. Knee surgery check-up; the unpleasant bite of life: temperamental ligaments. He waves and he is gone.

I admit to being both impressed and disturbed by Professor Von Ludwig – for the simple reason that he seemed to me a persuasive and wise old man who just happened to talk too much. But that is not the only reason: our brief exchange, I felt, exposed in me a spinelessness I never thought I possessed – ideological cowardice – the worst kind of deficiency anyone could be afflicted by. So glaring was my lack of personal grounding that I found myself easily charmed and seduced by people with the feeblest arguments or the most elementary observations. I'd always thought of poetry as my ticket out of this morass, the only way to imagine and record the inner worlds of the world. Philosophy was simply too dangerous for me at that time, for it would compel me to swim in the hallowed mental rivers of Aristotle and Plato and others in which I was convinced I would drown. I needed an ideology of my own, a shield against being completely obliterated by ancient but resilient ideas that have greatly shaped the present world. But, again, another thought cast shadows in my being: maybe philosophy could never be dangerous. One simply had to ignore it, think about something else: ice cream, stale bread, the sculpted shoulder blades of ugly women.

Twenty days pass. The queue at the Woolworths Food Market is long. I count thirty-three people, middle-class South Africans, drawn to a premium food range and packaging like flies to cow dung. The Carlswald Shopping Centre is intended for quick in-and-out shopping, but it seldom works that way because of the clogged parking and the hungers and errands of suburbia: post-office voyages, dry-cleaning collections, fast-food suicides, assaults on sobriety at the Poor Boys Pub. There are also stops at a D-grade dentist (an unrepent-ant inflictor of pain), visits to Kingsley, the ancient cobbler famous for resurrecting shoes, the goat's-milk outlet at shop L47, the humorous and borderline pervert florist James – he of the facial mole – as well as what should be the cleanest restrooms of any mall in the southern hemisphere. My groceries done (cereal, fruit, tomato sauce), I wait in line with a basket that gets heavier as I follow the winding queue to the tellers, my basket swallowing motoring magazines, slabs of dark chocolate, some nuts, an assortment of dried fruit, a copy of the *Sunday Times*, some marshmallows, four litres of Coca-Cola, and two cartons of milk. Some of the tellers are pretty – but average beauty, certainly not the kind that bewitches the senses, not the breed that suspends heartbeats.

Someone taps me on the shoulder:

Ah, my scholar. So you graze in these abundant fields too?

I am startled – first by the choice of words but also by a face that looks familiarly unfamiliar.

Von Ludwig, he says smiling, displaying perfect but tobacco-molested teeth.

Of course, I nod. I do graze in these fields, in this neighbour-hood.

Sunninghill man myself. I prefer living close to major motorways. It makes no philosophical sense searching for a highway before blasting off to whatever destination.

There's a pause, ever so brief.

So … have you decided what to do? The clock is ticking.

I haven't, actually, I confess in what I hope sounds a civil but grounded tone.

Choices, he says reflexively. The very act of choosing. I see you are a motoring enthusiast. I don't care much about automobiles myself. But put me butt naked in a Jacuzzi, with some red wine and some Nietzsche or Sartre, and I feel so alive and charged it feels as though I have flames coming out of my every orifice. Like a space rocket. The propulsion from old and new ideas – the collision between old and new wisdoms.

But I must admit, he continues as we shuffle forward a couple of centimetres, that there are times when not the finest wine rids me of an edgy feeling that true philosophy is in decline. Maybe it isn't. But we have to concede that television has contaminated global consciousness, as far as deep thinking is concerned.

Nine people stand between us and the pay points.

I want to be a poet, I remind him. He frowns, then smiles. Same difference, he says. Poetry is as in as much trouble as philosophy – for both are crafts of patience, some level of feeling. And that is near impossible in this age of moral drifters and artistic sadists.

There are six people in front of us now.

Besides, continues Von Ludwig, who says poetry needs to be written or memorised?

Three people left in the queue.

It can be argued, he shifts his basket to his left hand, that the totality of existence is poetry – or at least fragments of it. Have you seen the latest NASA images of Mars and distant planets – the colours, the scale and intricacy of beauty? What could that possibly be if not poetry? Or the grace and determination of a shooting star? A good and long marriage. Bird migrations en masse, or really beautiful toes on a stranger at a bus stop. Why should poetry – or even literature, written and spoken – pretend it has an upper hand on life as it is lived, with all its charms and horrors? Philosophy still has the upper hand, for thoughts are endless and countless things.

We part briefly as we reach the tills. I pay, he pays, and we make our way out into a light drizzle. Rain in the afternoon sun.

See, says he, poetry is not some abstract or random occurrence. It is sewn into the very essence of life. You only need to be born to be a poet. Nothing more. But that's a philosopher's mind talking – not that of an artist or scientist. Classic Foucault, sir, your desire to become a poet. Self-discovery is inferior to self-invention, Michel Foucault teaches us.

He stops next to a BMW station wagon, old but loved.

German engineering, he says with a wink. Pure poetry.

I muse: there had been a single item in Von Ludwig's shopping basket. Mouthwash. That is, surely, not poetry, but insurance against bad breath. How disappointing, yet necessary.

I see lovers in love and in lust at coffee shops in the Woolworths precinct. Lovers rub noses, remove eyelashes that have strayed onto eyeballs (careful finger actions, rapid blowing into the eye, even some tongue sweeps of the afflicted eye), generally inhabit flirtatious worlds through selected touching and low-key giggles. There is a peculiar abundance in the ways in which some people live their lives, as though nothing they do or say would later warrant a confession, a dissection of the conscience, a suppression of certain blemishes of decency. There are all sorts of love on display here: young, smitten love, the ageing love of a pensioner handkerchief cleaning a runny nose of a delirious fossil spouse, a toddler beaming and chuckling in a pram to an industrious and tipsy mother, the love for a pet confirmed by a rather pricy dog collar, and the love or addiction to cigarettes by a man chain smoking while sipping whisky from a hip flask. Other loves that seem evident but cannot be confirmed are two goldfish almost colliding in a dimly lit aquarium, a head chef praising the rarity and precision of his knives, what seems like a bitter spinster consumed by the strange thrills of a crossword puzzle.

There is, to put it mildly, the problem of a fast-dwindling pension. I am repelled by the very real and yet false power I wielded over Somalis, Eritreans and others from other African states, haunted by the question I still cannot answer: who does Africa *belong* to? That it belongs to the Africans is to me not a sufficient answer – it is an old, tired one, subservient to the arrogance of immigration. My paralysis has been the knowledge that I cannot pretend that there are no borders, or that the essence of human beings is essentially sainthood. I have less than a hundred thousand to my name and less than ninety days to decide how I am going to live, to survive, without attending to immigration headaches. Poets are mostly paupers, rich only in spirit, says Von Ludwig. What is the use of being important critically acclaimed and magical if you are also beautiful and starving asks Von Ludwig. Isn't the life of a bus driver or ticket inspector much more dignified – with the predictability of an income? And isn't this cowardice, this insistence on a structured life, a sentiment Michael K would probably have frowned upon? He had ceased being a gardener so why had it taken me so long to walk out of my grand office with its precarious powers, powers to preside over the lives of immigrants?

There are real emotional and existential costs to be expected from my dwindling pension. Sensual ones too. I have, over time learnt that sensuality cannot coexist with discomfort of any kind, that life's pleasures, however small or insignificant, are memorable only if nothing happens to alter the balance and purity of that pleasure. In other words, a police siren cannot coexist with a blowjob at the side of a motorway; a selfless and pleasant neighbour discovered to be a rehabilitated paedophile cannot be completely thought of as harmless – just as the temporary freedom of an escaped prisoner is fraught with suspicion and paranoia, just as there is only frustration in worshipping music if one does not have the talent to create it. The discomfort and later downright terror of not having money will expose me as not being equal to even the remotest association with Michael K – for I cannot stand the thought of not treating myself to the odd French art film, to savouring the love and romance and intrigue in subtitles, sitting down for a latte while perusing the most recent edition of an architecture magazine when there is the prospect of me having to feel my way to the toilet or my bed because the electricity has been cut off. There is no escaping the vindictive righteousness felt and dramatised by underpaid tellers and petrol attendants when money is short, a gradual deterioration in the plurality and aesthetics of shoes and underwear (to say nothing of cologne!), the inability to attend to such mundane matters as a haircut or money for a traffic fine. Elaborate planning will soon become necessary – thinking about and committing to paper or memory things that are important and mandatory, but also those that are equally important but not life-and-death necessities, weighing and counter-weighing the existential worth of a television set versus a groomed garden, a night at the theatre against a dignified pair of shoes, or a pricy birthday gift for a cherished lover in place of a potential appendix surgery. This means that I will become a different person, thrifty and cautious, two things that go totally against my nature.

I cannot help thinking, then, that I might have mistaken the awakening of *conscience* for urges of *art*, for a hungering thirst to enter the world of literature – a world, says Professor Von Ludwig, that has mauled and deformed many, driven some to insanity over the centuries. When asked by that fanatic philosopher Von Ludwig why I was so obsessed with becoming a poet, I answered: to calm my soul. He frowned, said true poetry had the opposite effect, that of stirring and impaling souls, setting things ablaze. Poets, true poets, poets born with verse in their kidneys, whose every breath seems perfumed with depth and eternity, suffer all manner of persecutions, their lives fraught with turbulence from either obscurity or too much fame, which tames the true claws of poetry. For poetry is supposed to wound you – small pleasurable cuts and gaping furrows, arrows shot through every pore, electrocuting the tiniest tip of every hair.

It struck me: how did one nurse (for friendships are, in their true nature, ailing things) a genuine friendship with a man who offered and expected nothing – who, even in the face of great turmoil, chose indifference and solitude over countless waves of the varied emotions bestowed on humans? What power, the discounting of those emotions, holding them at bay, as present but unnecessary. What could be more exhausting than following footprints that fade and reappear at random, that suggest a hallowed journey besieged by thorns and drought? And if ever there was a water well along the way, it reeked of urine! I mistook Michael K to be a mirror, only he wasn't; perhaps he was but that black spot on shattered mirrors, that point of impact that has lost its reflective powers, the damaged spot that holds together a mosaic of shattered glass, glass that has ceased to be a mirror, that distorts that which it is meant reflect into countless duplications, contortions of a damaged image. The broken mirror is dangerous, unreliable, armed with wound-inflicting shards, has a life that has become fragile, destined to shatter into a heap of vengeful glass. Perhaps Michael Ks are not mirrors – shattered or whole – but the wooden frames that house mirrors, prone to dust and roaches, to dust mites and cobwebs. There is yet another possibility, or question: was it possible that Michael Ks are such burrowers, so decapitated from humanity, that they cannot mirror its shadows and images? Perhaps each shattered fragment, too small to contain an image, is the new way of seeing – beauty in incoherence, a nudge towards the sanctity of portions of things, the comfort but suicide of not knowing. Terrifyingly, haven't rivers, lakes and ponds reflected passing things in distortions for as long as there have been eyes to see, a moment to notice? Haven't still waters mirrored branches of trees, birds flying by, even clouds? Do reflections have to mean anything if so many go unnoticed? Strangely, mirrors and rivers remain mute and unaffected by that that they reflect, allowing all manner of fleeting and pensive gazes over the centuries. Michael Ks: what of living, breathing, feeling and obscure mirrors – at once whole and shattered into a trillion microscopic particles of glass?

The professor invites me for coffee – which turns out not to be coffee but avalanches of wine and cheese. You could say we have become acquaintances, Kappus and Rilke of sorts. The Von Ludwig residence is not palatial, not an abode for a pauper either, but a charismatic apartment at Sunninghill's Blue Mist Estates, resident to rich folk and

those armed with foreign currency: Swedish telecommunications exec-
utives, Bristol dentists, Israeli-born surgeons and at least one Pakistani
mathematician. Rental is prohibitive, says Von Ludwig, security tight
and intrusive, the mood secluded and quiet. He lives alone, has
admirable taste in furniture, an impressive library and a fine wine
collection. He leads an uncomplicated life; apart from his obligations at
the university, he cooks, cleans, drinks wine and reads. He has procured
one of those massive flat-screen television sets, but it remains secured
in its box for he has come to the conclusion that television is toxic to
the life of the mind. His shelves house a healthy dose of German poets:
Brecht, Hebbel, Herta and Heiner Müller, Von Kleist and tens of others.

I am cautious but firm in pointing out Von Ludwig's apparently
limited source base, especially for someone with such firm opinions
on the matter of poets and poetry, of art and literature.

You seem to suggest that poets who matter are German – that
everything you know about the art form has German roots? No
sir. That would make me a gossiper and not a scholar. It is true
that I have, quite naturally, been exposed to the German poets, yes
but also to poets who travelled, intermarried, studied and had feuds
and friendships with Norwegians, Americans, and British folk, with
countless others from other lands. How do you think I ended up in
Johannesburg, sir? My rendezvous with literary minds, so to speak.

He teases me: 'I love you as certain dark things are to be loved, in
secret, between the shadow and the soul.' A pause. 'A wind is ruffling
the tawny pelt of Africa. Kikuyu, quick as flies, Batten upon the
bloodstreams of the velt. Corpses are scattered through a paradise
…' Pablo Neruda and Derek Walcott, respectively.

I nod, slightly embarrassed.

What you think you want is too late to want anyway, for even
if you do make it, you will be lonelier than the loneliest pollen dust

snatched from flowers by a fleeting breeze, never seen and trampled underfoot ... Who will be your contemporaries, who will read you? Don't you see how you will stick out like a Nazi in Jerusalem? It is not being a poet that you want. I know it seems so, that you have counselled and convinced yourself that poetry is your refuge. I am afraid it isn't so. It never was. And I should know. I know. I was born, burst my adolescent pimples and observed distant traces of pubic hair among poets, sir; walked dogs of poets, answered 'uncle' to poets, sniffed bed sheets of poets after tumultuous siesta debauchery. I have supported drunk poets home – too drunk for speech or locomotion, cautioned them against cursing God and screaming for the whole town to hear that their wives have uninspiring pleasure pots. I have stood at the graves of poets, witnessed them buried with biblical and poetic verse, so close to their caskets that I could smell a trace, a hint of their departed souls. I have visited ailing poets afflicted by all manner of misfortunes that befall humans at palatial and pitiful hospitals, rubbed their aching feet and, to their amusement and disgust, read them poetry by former lovers or rivals. I have babysat offspring of esteemed poets – some of whom have grown either to make millions managing manure companies or a pittance in obscure punk bands in Prague. I have found solace and outrage in poets, attended weddings where the purity of the verse for vows eclipsed entirely any kiss or honeymoon or happy marriage or growing-old-together story anyone could have dreamed or wished for. I have rescued poetry manuscripts from the hands of arsonists ... I know the value of poems in theory and practice, in perception and in degree of loss. I have been cursed by poets, lied to by poets, kicked in the groin by poets. I have given advice to poets revered as gods in certain circles – seen their eyes harden and soften in disbelief, their tear ducts surrender to unexpected insight from a would-be kindred spirit. I have, best of all, my beloved sir, had the timeless and rarest privilege of disrobing poets – youngish and adventurous ones between the ages of twenty and the fringes of thirty, and mature dames with friendly frowns and muted gasps, women with devastating nude profiles and wine breath, who composed poetry in the crack of dawn, who rested on my chest or bare buttocks as I slumbered in contentment, reserved for bearers of secrets and erotic muses. In Berlin. Frankfurt. In selected and rare private lodgings in Zurich. I have, my esteemed sir, pruned rose bushes belonging to arrogant poets, inherited priceless thoughts stopped in their tracks by death and disease. I have had my juvenile rantings, insolent and shameful behaviour blunted, later sharpened and polished by poets so talented they could sniff out closet poets by how they sipped their coffee: poets from within the family, visiting poets from other provinces, poets in mourning encountered at the burial sites of other more famous poets. I have been betrayed by poets, witnessed the decline of once great ones splinter into twigs of doubt and despair – for poetry is a soul and not mind thing!

I am dumbfounded by the passion and eloquence of his liaisons with poets.

And so it is that I tell him about Michael K.

I respect your being intrigued and bewildered by your friend Michael K, he answers. But if he was as detached as you say he was, it seems to me that what you think you had was a one-sided friendship. Friends share passions: love for horses, admiration for jazz trumpeters, panty sniffers who worship in the dark and furthest frontiers of the internet, master wine blenders, daredevils, skirt chasers of varied temperaments, and washed-out men through whose mouth beers of the world flow. Friendships are anchored around such things, such connections. And you are telling me that this Michael K of yours never squeezed a single tit in his entire life, never held a baby in his arms, grew and fed on pumpkins? That his claim to fame is surviving war camps, where he was a lazy bum anyways and an object of pity – a charity case most of his life? What did you talk about with this Michael K of yours? Surely, stories about war and a dead mother should have run cold and got stale within the first week of the friendship? And then what ...? I, with respect, for not having met or seen your friend even from a distance, without sounding too hasty and judgemental, think that you are placing far too much value on this Michael K of yours.

He is serious now.

Are you not mistaking a recluse for a simple transmitter of grand ideas, ideas that should have rusted by now? He was a gardener, his mother died, he was in hiding, was arrested, escaped. My question is: *so what?* Why should you or anyone care that he built a pyramid or that a famous Nobel laureate came to bury him? Or, let me put it this way, except for some theoretical pretences on the ownership and manner of one's God-given life, has Michael K contributed in any significant way to South Africa – and don't tell me his life and ways are an allegory! Such escape routes belong in lecture theatres, not in real life. Which brings me to my earlier point, why – and I could be wrong – I don't believe you are wired to take part in the caresses and decapitations of poetry, that you can truly march to the war drum of poetry. For that drum is a call to arms like none you have either seen or imagined. I am not talking small skirmishes here, Miles, but wars of the soul, to safeguard its elusive tranquillity; these are the most heart-numbing and least expected.

The legion of real poets is beyond blood oaths, sir. It is sealed by releasing portions of one's breath into the firmament, where it will hover for a lifetime in search of words and timelessness. I am not saying you cannot be a poet – I am merely cautioning you. Poetry sir, is not only rhyme, not just words on a page. You will find with time, or by succumbing to its subtle dictatorships, that it is a never-ending harvesting of the human soul, a relentless search for every place it has ever been, how it has been stirred and strangled, cajoled and patted, left to bloom: in faraway islands, in lonesome retreats up eerie mountain spires, in shadows left by obsolete yearnings, the oppressive moral weight of whorehouses at the crack of dawn. You will find that if you looked into your very being, not through fleeting glances or restless gazes, but that disrespectful and creepy stare that prompts discomfort, lingering triumphs and disasters of generations or entire civilisations. That, sir, is the true power of thought, and not of poetry. Poetry merely records these things. And you are saying to me you want to dwell on ruins, when things have happened, when people have lived and perished; that you want to be a poet, a vulture, gliding above wastelands below, biding time, waiting for an opportunity for the stench of dead and dying things, for you to swoop down, sharp-beaked, and scavenge? What is so original about that?

He did not wait for an answer.

The world of thoughts on the other hand, my dear sir, can remain as fresh as dewdrops – free of contaminants, stripped of familiarity.

Maybe, I think to myself, Michael Ks – if there is ever truly more than one – do not belong to an age. So guarded are their lives and private passions that they escape scrutiny, thwart comparisons, cannot be quantified. That discreet power to subvert the known world, the indifference to its demands and madness, is perhaps a much more powerful possession than the gift of poetry, for unlike his equally guarded friend, John Coetzee of the Land Cruiser, Michael K never expressed or feigned any interest in Keats or Byron, and yet, said Professor Gikandi, secured obscure fame by existing against existence. What poem could possibly be greater than that: passing a cursory look at life, emptying one's bladder on its fledgling seedlings? What verse possesses sufficient magic to distort time, live outside of its arousals? For time has proven itself to be both kind and spiteful, but most of all sensual, in how it goes about its charms and coercions, how it rearranges or discards whole lives, the uncertainty it imposes on known but unproven possibilities. Was it not a mistake then to elevate poets to literary deities when all they recorded was life in its limitations, its known deceptions? Shouldn't such status thus be bestowed on Michael Ks rather – those immune to the sensations of rhyme and artificial images? For a bird on a page, described in ink, can never truly be a bird, chirpy and twitching, with warm blood coursing its veins; a flower in paper and ink has a scent that can be nothing but false, it can never possess the immediacy of bees and powdery pollen, the splendour of the afternoon sun, for instance.

Not even powerful legislators can completely contain or govern human nature, says Professor Von Ludwig. That which we have come to know and accept as life is in fact acceptable and disturbing spillages of our restless natures: divorces, executions, revolutions, erotic espionage, acts of treason, the shaky pillars of hope and faith, other countless life irritants.

So it is that I, the more I read about the lives and works of poets – some of whom have aged and deceased – realise the full magnitude of my desired life as poet. I am electrified by the arresting power of language, the tingling sensations that trip down the spine when in the claws or affections of an accomplished poem, the myriad projectiles of feeling that threaten to excavate yearnings long entombed, the product of a lifetime of slavery to words and their shadows. I know that those arid or scorched lines do not grow on trees, that the captivating musings of poets that linger and hide under the tongue, that continue to preoccupy literature professors and readers, capable of poisoning or redeeming souls, are in essence the surest way to a life of a recluse, a day dreamer fixed on the precise manner with which dresses flutter in the breeze, how butterflies congregate among reeds on crystal lakes. That such instincts, to observe and record one-hundred-thousandth of the tail end of a second, the immediacy of sudden light, take lifetimes to possess and exploit. What chance did I have, I whose life had already consumed half a century and is headed for turbulence associated with lives of paupers and men fortunate enough to be on the priority lists of assassins?

The one thing that truly stands out, that I cannot hide or do anything about is of course my eyes. I have big eyes, as you can see, big vision balls swimming in salty liquid, tears that have forced me to own handkerchiefs to guard against sudden spillages when I am hurt or deeply moved. There is a deceptive vacuousness to my eyes, an unthreatening calm that is pleasing and yet misleading, how my eyes can, for instance, look into a toddler's without triggering alarm, how little they reflect of the inner workings of my soul. This is not to say I possess dead, unexpressive eyes, without beauty or personality, but rather that such descriptions remain elusive, mainly because of the distant gaze I have mastered over the years. It is not true that eyes are windows to the soul; I am living proof of that. For vain and conventional people, maybe, but not for me.

I could, when my thoughts drifted, see from my office windows the temperament and inner workings of clouds – when they were snow-white patches drifting across the sky as if in oblivion, when they became irritated light-grey smoky pebbles dotting the firmament, when they evolved into moody crooked lines and darkening shapes that changed from agitation to creeping fury – that chilled the air and ushered in sudden winds and a dimming of light that prompted the trembling of senses from distant and approaching thunder roars. There was in my thoughts, in that moment of the storm seen through a six-by-four window, a sense that there was an entirely different life – a life of the high heavens – that remained disconnected and unaffected by the perils of democracy, by human bodies rising and falling in the expansive oceans of nobility and wretchedness, in Johannesburg's precarious beauty. I suspect my boss had dashing looks in her youth. There were still traces: the curve of her legs, the kissable mouth, the ears that made earrings look good, her disarming smile. But those looks had been dealt a severe blow by age and hard work, so severe that she looked like a distant rendering of what beauty was supposed to be, only faded, assaulted, but resilient. I would not have married my boss, for she belonged to that group of women who aged badly, features all but collapsed, a double chin that threatened a triple chin, and smoky eyes that projected nobility and a dash of calculated deceit. A layer of fat covered her elbows, her teeth a creaming white, her breath hinting at traces of fumigation chemicals.

I had in my time dismissed a few seemingly upright colleagues for preying on immigrants: taking bribes, breaking the law. I was unpopular, I know, but remained defiant to the very last, telling the bigoted lizards in management: immigrants are people and not your playthings – behave! Office decorum muzzled me from firing arrows that stung my heart, so I cursed them when solitary – in the toilet, in elevators, in the car in gridlock traffic, in the shower, in the underground parking – hissing: donkeys, heartless brutes, inhumane fuck balls, xenophobic zealots, soulless sadists, assassins of hope! But someone must have been listening to my enraged heart, for my memos went missing, my Volvo was keyed and headlights vandalised with a brick in the underground parking. That silent war spilled into my coffee mug going missing (who do you ask when everyone is sullen and toxic?), colleagues developing sudden chronic ailments and skipping important meetings, and the gremlins from Finance delaying life-and-death payments.

I was, the day I received the letter confirming my upward adjustment in wages, besieged by an erratic bout of nausea. I, the esteemed director-general, whose life purpose seems to have withered into meagre pickings, who had become an outsider looking in, at papers stamped and signed, raining whip lashes on the souls of fellow Africans. The drive home was not without its tragedies. I was stopped at a police roadblock, issued a traffic fine for driving a vehicle with shattered headlights.

What have we here, asked the most impatient and agitated policeman I have ever encountered. I explained that I was having problems with faceless colleagues at the office.

Ja, but what do office catfights have to do with your responsibility to drive a roadworthy automobile?

I agree. But this happened sometime this afternoon. Someone smashed my lights and I know exactly who it was too.

Ja, but then that ceases to be office quarrels and a case of arson and damage to property – in which case you have a duty to report the matter to the police.

My eyes followed him as he circled my Volvo and there, on the passenger door, silver lettering had been carved into the metal with a knife or some other sharp object, succinct in its judgement: *Traitor!*

And? asks the officer. What is this about?

I lifted and dropped my shoulders in shock and bewilderment.

I might have outgrown my own life, I said feebly.

This is dangerous, whatever it is. Again: report the matter to the police, sir. Or do I need to arrest you for laziness?

Maybe. But how do you police savagery?

Look, I don't know what you mean, what savagery you're talking about. You get those lights replaced. You cannot by law and common sense be driving blind, whatever your explanations. I man roadblocks, weed out bad elements. That's all. Now please feel free to proceed on your trip.

I thought: how inadequate, how routine, how shallow. How was I to tell the officer – whatever his name was – what happened to my father?

DUST ISLAND / JOHANNESBURG

Dust Island does not appear on any map of South Africa (not all places populated by people and other living things are indicated on maps). A back-of-beyond outpost ideal for self-discovery and fugitives, it was an accidental discovery – the end point of an aimless road trip across three provinces, across an expansive, barren, yet soul-stirring Karoo to the furthest territorial shadows of Cape Town. It was never for the sake of poetry or self-discovery or a spur-of-the-moment road trip that, after erratic days of motel living and hitch-hiking in search of a place tranquil and remote, I stumbled across Dust Island. Life had become claustrophobic, edgy, insecure; I had become terrified of mailboxes, of mail, of tomato sauce. I had had eerie premonitions that an assassin lurked, waiting for me to collect my mail.

And so it was that what was meant to be a two-month hideout congealed into a three-year haze, a distortion of time and character. It did not help that that delicate balance of trying to restore a tattered soul, a soul dipped in the corrosive waters of a mid-life crisis, the war between self-preservation and reckless anger, radiated, shockwaves from my suspended monumental mourning, the memory of that crime scene, my father face down, lifeless, his shoes polished and laces tied, his corpse exemplary in fashion and personal-grooming precisions.

I must admit to, when my mind didn't drift to other planets, or recoil into knots, being seduced by sights and scenes on my road trip: butterflies of all hues and sizes perching on welcoming flowers, sunrays bouncing off black stones in darkened splendour, curious dogs that sniffed Johannesburg scents on my heels as I checked into privately owned B&Bs, and a very distant throb of lust awakened by a brief copulation scene in some political drama, the title and details of which I never established beyond being alerted to the raw charge with which the female love interest, Mary Anne, dictated to the docile would-be intercourse partner saying: Forget the bed. I strictly get pleasured on staircases: the discomfort, the risk of injury, bruises inflicted by wanton passion are medals worth having for something so sense-imploding. I went to bed thinking about staircases, and have never looked at the toils of architects in the same way since.

So you can imagine my apprehension and despair at present, every time Maureen makes her way up and down my apartment staircase. I must look tortured, for she always politely asks whether everything is all right, to which I answer with an affirmative nod. I avoid newspapers, those that carry images of the scene of my father's murder, editorials on forensic investigations into Russian roulette games played by civil servants with state funds. Isn't it amazing, I think, that freedom turned stale so quickly, became con-taminated by mould, from nefarious acts that breed moral rats and roaches in the dark, that blight the Republic with conscience leprosies of the fatal kind?

Professor Von Ludwig is carefree with his visits to me, never informs me when he is on his way or even that he intends coming. The buzzer simply chimes its melody and a lively voice says: I come bearing poetry. The same line is much repeated, dozens and dozens of times, and with it comes countless books by poets and about poets, for poets on six continents. He also, without fail, brings me all manner of Woolworths fruit and, again without fail, gives me tight and long hugs as though trying to squeeze every ounce of breath out of me. He is a man of compliments, of ready laughter, of gentle discreet encouragements. There are times, even though we speak almost every second day on the telephone, when I wish the buzzer would ring, when it has gone for a week or two without ringing.

Today's buzz is followed by a naughty chuckle and something new: I have taken the liberty to top my poetry shipments with a poem on two gorgeous legs and a brain to disturb gravity. I am in the company of a lady, sir, so hide any embarrassing artefacts that might be in view. But there is nothing embarrassing. Maureen always makes sure of that, ensures that not even a teaspoon is out of place. Upon arrival, Von Ludwig places fruit on the table, some Edgar Poe and Marechera titles, noting which I frown.

Anything wrong?

No. Nothing's wrong. But I am running out of shelf space.

Nonsense. Poetry is a world of abundance, don't you know? His is a wry smile.

And, by the way, this lovely lady with me is Boitumelo, whom I have irreversible intentions to marry.

I nod, smile. I am Miles. It's a great pleasure to meet you. This here is Maureen. She helps me seem clean and orderly. Maureen, please meet Boitumelo, Professor Von Ludwig's future wife.

Maureen and Boitumelo retreat to the lounge, settle in front of the television. The spine on the Marechera book reads *Cemetery of Mind*. Odd, I think, but weighty.

You really need a woman in your life, Miles, says Von Ludwig. Where is your fire going to come from if you exist by your lonesome? Poets thrive on romantic bliss, on marital warfare. So what if your first marriage dwindled into nothing? You can always marry again. What about her, your helper? She's a competent candidate, is she not?

She is a child, man. Besides, our relationship is strictly professional.

Although this, of course, was not strictly true: I so desired Maureen that at times I temporarily lost my mind, any sense of restraint. That I imagined, with a sudden swell of emotions and enlightenment, how desperately I craved Greek salad: cucumbers, lettuce, onion rings and baby tomatoes, only dressed with her springs, her womanly eruptions resultant from our imagined carnal sieges. I, on occasions, at obscure restaurants, still order Greek salad for its erotic rather than dietary qualities – and, when salad dressings are presented as options, wish Maureen was around to squat over the bowl, let loose precious leaks. That I would pounce on her and show her that the devil existed, and when she moaned and fluttered, regain my composure by feasting on my salad she would have been too kind to irrigate. What could be profounder than that where I literally and figuratively ate her, *ingested* her mysterious waters, used her panties as a napkin?

Lovely Boitumelo, Von Ludwig lures me back: her eyes are a specific white – not as white as milk or snow or show pigeons, but the white of clouds not contaminated by smoke or rainwater or the shadows of other clouds. It seems to me that her soul has the same cloud quality – clouds as seen from forty thousand feet from aircraft windows: some convoluted bales of nothingness, some uncertain and orphaned dots wandering the sky, others impressions of surefooted, beautiful and commanding mountain ranges in bursts of angry reds and bluish purples. There is an expansiveness about her inner life, a sense of elusiveness that can, like the clouds, alter form and movement, that can dominate without really being there. I love her for her simple tastes – tea rituals, walks in the gardens.

Tell that to a famished heart, I say. I really believe that a famished gaze will make you a poet – or a better one, if you don't turn out to be atrocious with verse.

We burst out laughing, startle Maureen and Boitumelo.

Von Ludwig composes himself: About your friend. Did you know there's a book about him? A famous book.

What friend?

That Michael fellow. There's a book about him. I haven't read it yet, but thought that it might be of interest to you.

A book?

Yes, a book. And lots of papers and other books from all manner of scholars about the book.

Scholars are investing time and effort scrutinising a vagabond? I ask.

Yes. It also seems to me that they will continue to do so into the foreseeable future.

Michael never mentioned anything of the sort to me. I doubt he knew of such.

Well, some people exist in bubbles.

Maybe it's not the same Michael. Michael is a common name.

It is, from what you have told me, the same Michael, I can assure you.

Have you seen a copy of this book?

Not with my own eyes, not yet, but it exists.

An autobiography?

No, no. A novel. Isn't it strange that your friend seems to be so shrouded in myth? The little that I perused, reviews and things, project quite an interesting specimen of almost mythical proportions. It seems to me that the person you met is identical to the one written about in this book. Vacuous. Elusive. Unyielding. But there is, philosophically speaking, inherent danger there: overthinking and being misled by the fictional and real lives of strangers. Recluses are perpetual strangers. Some are valuable, perhaps, but the greater questions are: to whom, to what end, is this value? Can you touch it, mould it into bricks and mortar to shelter the homeless? If not, what is the point?

Von Ludwig lowers his voice a decibel or two, to almost a whisper.

Can you imagine someone as alluring, as pleasing to the eye and heart as my Boitumelo being a tortured recluse? That would be a waste, wouldn't it? Maybe you will be a poet for the suffering, my friend, for the profound and misunderstood.

We laugh.

Michael never once mentioned anything being written about him – which is in itself not surprising, but somewhat odd. Even recluses, surely, must have crumbs of vanity. Moments of navel gazing. Some splinter of arrogance, of self-worth?

Remember, I am a scholar, Miles, so I have certain standards to uphold. Worse for me – philosophy places most of those standards out of reach. Surgeons operate on cancers; patients live or die. One plus one is two for mathematicians. A bus driver has predetermined stops and a specific routine. Not so with philosophy and science. That which isn't known is always the more interesting, but elusive. Eat your strawberries, sir. The cream is melting, he says. So ... what are you going to do for money? Starving poet languishing in garrets and all that ...

I don't know. I'll see.

Is it that bad – that you would abandon your work without a plan? Humans are naturally competitive, some unpleasant – no?

It's not only that. Mine is a problem of conscience, which I suppose trumps all material comforts you can think of. I ask myself: who does Africa belong to?

But isn't that a rhetorical question? It belongs to the Africans, and others, just as America and France belong, to some extent, to Germans, Spaniards, Croatians and others. I have heard your point about immigration injustices – heard it many times – but what do you think should happen? You are not advocating for a lawless country, are you? For all manner of unsavoury characters to come and go as they please? That is dangerous idealism, surely!

No. That's not my point. Mine is a problem of conscience and an awakening of art in me. That's all. I might never be a poet. That too is all right with me. I will find something else to do. I might, of course, also be a dead man walking – so that is also very sobering.

No one will hurt you. You are just traumatised by all those refugee papers and heart-rending scenes, that's all. You haven't exposed anyone. You walked away.

You don't have much time.

I know.

Boitumelo reminds Von Ludwig she has a dentist appointment and that ends their visit.

There are times when it feels like my soul has crystallised, hardened into rock before shattering into a million pieces, each fragment a distant quavering of a misplaced feeling – collisions of feelings old and new, in a state of paralysis. There is a sense of an impending implosion – fast-approaching – where my entire life would collapse into a haunting echo, evidence of fleeting and disappearing things, of present but intangible things. It is not decay, not quite destruction, but a cold shadow of an existence that has become burdensome and insecure. It is at the very last moments of the approaching implosion that everything is halted, returns to eerie normalcy, fragile and silent. I have fortified my defences against the slow erosion of a man I imagined I would become – an exemplary civil servant, before such ambitions were assassinated by a sudden reawakening: that the state was crawling with dynasties and allegiances of rats, humans that had suddenly grown fur, teeth that nibbled into every crevice of our lives. These were not rats that lived on garbage heaps or in sewers, no, sir: but suited and perfumed rodents with invisible tails. How well they hid their fur, the rats, how skilfully they detected footsteps and light, how they could blend into the shadows.

I spend hours on the balcony, edgy and unshaven, Maureen feeding me anything from fruit to wine. I quench the soul with some Walcott and Krog, some Kgositsile, who wrote about digging graves with artistic precision. The balcony view is of Midrand and its surrounds, Johannesburg with its sloping hills, the Mike One Highway that connects Johannesburg and Pretoria, of on- and off-ramps to and from the Edens, cemeteries and wastelands of suburbia. It is as if the verse lifts off the page, as though individual words float from Von Ludwig's books, from the ancient and nascent souls of poets into the night sky, hovering as if in curling smoke destined skywards, with the grace and mystery of mist on a windless day. Poets keep me company on the balcony, some in the front passenger seat, others invited to my long, foamy baths that seem to last for eternity.

The telephone calls, between Von Ludwig and I, seem ritualistic medicinal, as he educates me on the nuances and tantrums of poets He says I must remind him to, when the poetry has seeped into the bone marrow, procure me some Balzac or Marías, initiate and preserve me into the cathedrals of prose. Whereas most blazes of poetry burn straight to the heart, says Von Ludwig, the infernos of prose are wildfires of being.

You should invest some evenings in Uhlmann and Zamyatin some Vizinczey, he says, and imbibe some Julian Barnes with the knowledge that there existed a Mr Vonnegut and there exists a Mr Okri in the universe. That Dr Angelou's words will continue to be atomic, to bloom as flowers yet to be discovered, bloom to the breeze of Bellow and Head. Then, he says, we have to – depending on what you become, for literature changes you – expose you to the horizons of Foucault and Žižek, to the private gardens of Derrida and bell hooks. And yet, he warns, it is not ideal to be completely lost in the world of books, for it is not possible to be whole in the refuge of art, of ideas; there is living to be done, living that can be abundant and bittersweet, that can be foggy and unkind, that can be searing and bruising, that can maim and impale, be both meagre and profound. We have to remember to live among flesh-and-blood people – including living poets and descendants of poets – which of course we do: in the bars and bistros of Melville and Newtown; to marvel at the beautiful, twisted and lucid minds of artists at the Goodman and Johannesburg art galleries, unwind at the coffee havens of Woodmead and Bedfordview, lust ignited and molten in the hot-air-ballooning escapades of Muldersdrift. All this we do – and more – and, in the process, become kindred spirits.

Von Ludwig does not understand that I have only ever loved one woman – loved her all the more when she loved and permitted love from men everyone agreed to be less than me, when she married and divorced and remarried in a decade and half-sobbed into the telephone line from faraway hotel rooms or on my shoulder. That I loved her with the knowledge that she loved me, but that it was possible for other kinds of love never to bloom to their full splendour, to fold themselves into cocoons of utter silence. Von Ludwig says he understands but does not agree with such a commitment to old and unavailable love – given that the universe was afloat with astonishingly gorgeous women. This is true, obviously: Maureen in my house, jovial waitresses with infectious smiles and giddy glances lowering teapots toward cups, the rank and file of fleeting faces with beguiling limbs and arresting perfumes at airport terminals and, better yet, flight attendants who have learnt to smile on command and to ignore aeroplane turbu-lence of the wickedest kind. But none are Palesa, coy but deadly in how she could promise a kiss that would arrive eleven years into the future with the immediacy of a beating heart. I loved and love the symmetry of her toes, the traces of pubescent hair when she had shaved her legs, the exact manner with which she averted her mouth whenever I attempted to time travel, when I couldn't bear the eleven-year sentence, the time it would take for me to confirm once and for all the supremacy of her kiss. I watched, instead, as time withdrew its affections on her figure, when motherhood domesticated and plundered her sparkling personality, when cohabitation with husbands dimmed the brilliance of her smile, when concealed betrayals sprang into view, clubbed to bloody death the little girl whose spirit played violins, leaving a sobbing beloved with drooping breasts and dental fillings sobbing on the other end of hotel telephones.

I still tear up at the many needle pricks to my soul that I survived at the hands of Palesa – small and unintentional cruelties. I don't think she ever fully understood that every hair end in my body electrocuted me the moment I laid eyes on her, that – at the promise of her love and embrace – I would still walk vast deserts and wastelands in search of a cure to that particular ailment that saw me seek other loves, difficult loves, my tendency to specialise in widows My heart was too laden with grand yearning and pathos to ever be content with fleeting and paper-thin romances. I was born for and courted difficult love. My accidental and deliberate excursions into the worlds of widows and widowhood proved exhausting. It soon became apparent that the kind of love one seeks, secures and nurtures from a widow is a far greater love – for the pathos it offers the finality with which even mundane matters are discussed and expressed. Unlike conventional romantic love, with the giddiness of fluttering hearts, love from and of a widow is a serious paradox. Apart from the ever-present shadow of the dead husband, his house, cars and clothes and sometimes children, his photographs in life and in ill health, in death, the noble things he was loved and is missed for (cooking, brutal honesty, generosity with gifts and not money), grief ushers for the woman in mourning, whether one or three years after the burial, a new lease on life. To walk into such an arrangement, of a disrupted life, of tarnished hopes, of eternal pain inflicted by sudden loss, is to take upon oneself the daunting duty of being a custodian of tear ducts – and, for the most fragile, a constant companion at hospital wards. Walking into such stirring emotions is to commit to having a boundless heart, not easily moved by unjustifiable emotional outbursts and comparisons with a dead husband: Matthews would have never jumped to conclusions; he would have sought my opinion. Or: I know you are trying – and I appreciate that – but it is just not the same. I commend you for being the man you are, but Milton was in another league, the King of My Castle. It means ignoring temperamental children, whose rude and inconsiderate antics place the death of the father squarely at your feet. It is a life of constant suspicion, of cold shoulders and unending judgement, twelve-year-old lashing: You are nothing like my father! Patriotism feels very much like that, like being in love with a widow, having to accept both thorny and delightful things past and present. To, not without a touch of caution, wonder why love for one's country, its peoples, can be so fraught with restraint and despair – modulated love, a love whose blossoming cannot be easily reached, love encircled then by barbed wire. It is the kind of love that punishes you for loving, an aloof kind of love, expansive but indifferent. A love that is prone to secrecy and manipulation, that offers no guarantees of dependability. A love that expects love without fully returning it.

That's not love, protests Von Ludwig.

What is it then?

He does not miss a beat: I am not sure of its kind or degree, but it is definitely madness.

We laugh. He continues to laugh. But that sinking feeling remains. It is as if a portion of my heart has combusted – that its microscopic life veins have been charred, leaving a crippled heart, defenceless against its own yearnings.

Aren't you tempted? he asks with a naughty aversion of direct eye contact, inspecting the carrot cake more than is believable or necessary.

I think for a moment, say: A little. But such temptations are mostly for strangers, are they not? So, statistically speaking, a large percentage of such women, no matter how catastrophically beautiful, either belong elsewhere or are oblivious to the suffering observer who dissects the most miniscule of their gestures.

That might be true, but isn't that a deprived view of life, especially for an aspirant poet?

No, it isn't. Depravity has nothing to do with it. It's a question of instincts, instincts that exist regardless of the goings-on in the world.

But what is instructive about who belongs to whom or who is oblivious to what?

There you go again, Von Ludwig. Not everything has to undergo philosophical scrutiny.

True. But is deep thought not kindred spirits with deep emotion, even when shrouded in doubt?

Can't we simply drink coffee in peace?

We laugh.

No, we cannot, he says. Not until someone leaves traces of feminine scent in your bed. You will be amazed how good that is to an ageing man. The belonging you spoke about. You cannot float around like a wine cork, sir. Poetry is about secrets – secrets hidden in plain sight, illuminated by what we think we know about the universe. Poets I knew, those I intended knowing, had one thing in common: inner lives, vulnerabilities.

Granted. But what do inner lives and vulnerabilities have to do with damaging love?

Nothing. Damaging love has everything to do with wanting the impossible, with self-pity – a very demeaning and self-defeating kind of relationship with oneself. Even if she threw loving arms around you – now, tomorrow morning – of what use will that love be if the vessel that holds it bears cracks, is in the process of destructing, or at least losing value?

That may be so, my philosopher friend, but who is to say, with certainty, that there is no value in cracks, in the passage of time?

An excellent point, I grant you, but of what use is calculating the value of cracks if you have no heart to contain that value? In other words, there is a real possibility of that value remaining worthless, for the true value of things lies in their form, their being whole, not in cracks.

I can tell that our sparring is challenging my opponent in ways he hadn't been able to predict. I can see in his guarded eyes that his mind is ticking over, steadily, methodically, determined to counter any argument of mine with an equally eloquent – if not more thoroughly considered – response. But I am not about to let up.

Insightful, Mr Philosopher, but how else are we to determine the value of things if we pretend it is possible to shield them against the passage of time? Isn't it true that time both illuminates and buries cracks in things? That without time the true value of things cannot be calculated? That cracks and imperfections are perhaps the very reasons some things become rare, priceless?

Too idealistic, even by philosophical standards. Is that a trace of vexation I detect in Von Ludwig's tone? Too far removed from real life. Humans do not readily embrace visible decay, whether in other humans or objects. This is why some take the lead in restoring a sense of normality to chaotic situations – a need to suppress rational thought, blunt it with spiritual concerns. Why else visit and pray for convicted rapists and murders? See? Everything is connected: small cracks that grow to cause unthinkable tremors, cracks that put in question the very idea of loving and valuing things.

What life-and-death point are you are making – all your thought entanglements considered?

Von Ludwig smiles. That's easy. You need a woman, a privilege woven in nature itself. Don't be a time bomb, overladen with human seeds … He sits back, arms folded, eyes narrowed. On a more serious note, though, my esteemed poet, not a word we have uttered means a thing if we are not able to tie it to the lives of flesh-and-blood people. The question is: what kind of poet do you intend becoming? For there are types, you know. Is it your wish to tickle your readers with a feather, with shallow charms, or do you intend bludgeoning them with blunt objects of truth? Let's face it, without being political, there are evident cracks in the vessel of freedom. This country will go to the dogs, as you always say. Politics might not save it. Poetry might be too distant an elixir. Spiritual preoccupations might engender numbing sleep while rats in three-piece suits plunder and maim. Humans with fur!

That's some insight, I tell Von Ludwig. I am, though not fanatical, a patriot, one weary and suspicious of the ashes of this country – with its rot and magnificence. One more word about apartheid and I am going to jump off the Burj Khalifa.

Not so fast, he says. Nations are imperfect things – made of all manner of terrors, big and small. I am, or used to be, German, remember? Which is not to say South Africa cannot outlast its plagues. Everything fades with time, sir. Everything.

I nod, smile.

And then we part. Sweet sorrow, it seems.

There are times when Von Ludwig travels – Peru, Amsterdam, Costa Rica; when he is away for a week or three on end, when I am totally lost and inconsolable. I despise it that my life has become so fragile, so eventless, so insecure. Coffee is not the same without him, and while he dazzles scholars and radio people as far as Algiers and Bucharest, I am left alone to arrest an increasingly rebellious soul. His poetry shipments have awakened new planets in me, spaces so far-reaching and new that the eyes flickers with curiosity and trepidation at cemeteries of the human soul, its magnificent lakes, its odours from blending with aspirant saints and wretches over time. A certain light seldom comes to illuminate the underwater caves that house secrets to the true nature of my soul – its murkiness and blinding faiths, beliefs in things pleasant and vile. There is a problem, though: that light takes too long to come – and when it does, it dims before the secrets of my soul can be uncovered, scrutinised, known.

I think of my time in the public service, about the hundreds of people I have come to know, about how we endured lacerations of the conscience, how hard we have fought to stop ourselves from growing fur, how we with clenched teeth resisted ever-growing tails, how vigilant and guarded we had all become in order to stop any of the ones that had grown fur and tails from biting us in the heels. And we walked – as some continue to walk – in the manicured gardens of our Republic, our ears pricked to detect the slightest sounds of those who had grown tails, plotting in their pungent swamps. Freedom means nothing if not jealously guarded, says Von Ludwig, for as we say during our coffee pilgrimages in and around the metropolis: some fur and tails grow on the inside; the most promising of crystal lakes at times leads to the most decaying of swamps.

When he returns, our reunion is inevitably a joyous one, supping at the oasis that is friendship, companionship. I have lost count how many times Von Ludwig has brought me gifts so I, out of shame, fondness and a sense of decency, procure him a steeply priced set of travel luggage at a reputable and exclusive Sandton City shop. The catalogue claims they are made of the finest, softest leather and have models in red Ferraris and Bentleys parked alongside private jets.

The last I spoke to him, Von Ludwig intimated he had left Stockholm and would connect back to South Africa via Zurich. I am looking forward to surprising him with the luggage set, even though the saleslady with defeated acne pimples said I had gone overboard in intending to gift someone such an expensive gift – that it was not her place to say so, but that she thought such a gift should be reserved for a spouse, or someone who has saved your life, without whom you would not be alive. I mentioned that Von Ludwig had in fact saved my life, to which she enquired if it was from a fight or a drowning, leaving me to chuckle at her forwardness and unguarded speculation.

My gift buying has spiked. I buy Von Ludwig cufflinks, an overpriced (collector's item) record player in polished mahogany within a week of each other, followed by objects associated with time and thinking: pendulums, landscape paintings, sculpture in wood and marble, a comfortable rocking chair apparently manufactured in Czechoslovakia in the 1960s, at least seven variations of hourglasses, crystal balls. I feel indebted to the man, not pressured debt, not the kind from which one lies awake, chewing nails. It gives me peculiar pleasure owning, embracing this debt of mine, for the worlds it uncovers, the thoughtful tears that collect in Von Ludwig's eyes. I am amazed at how much of a shopper this undeclared debt has made me how I am able to sift through stalls and stalls at curio shops and spot the most immaculate gift, how to bestow pricelessness on otherwise mundane artefacts, how I wrestle my bank account like a matador in doubt. There are times when I feel graceful, so touched by our brotherly coffee voyages, our poetry recitals, that I could volunteer to rip my kidneys out of my body, wrap them in white gold foil, present them to Von Ludwig with a bow.

Von Ludwig will, if all goes well, land on a Swiss Air flight by mid-morning tomorrow, and we will have our ritual airport coffee while he sketches goings-on on his trip from memory and out of a sense of treasured accomplishment. The man is valued for his ideas – for illuminating the ideas of others, for wondering out loud whether trees feel pain, whether that would change our view of the world if it were confirmed that they did. All the mass murders in tropical forests, all the axes and wildfires, all the broken spines from storms, their shame of being urinated upon by dogs and men, the countless crucifixions and maimings as trees are tortured and moulded into furniture, pain from hail assaults, electrocutions from overhead power cables and lightning, wounds from stray bullets, fractures from overturning automobiles, those silent drownings from flash floods. That would turn life on its head, won't it, he asks, learning and confirming that trees feel pain – the buttocks of girls rammed against tree trunks by horny men, sudden assassinations from earthquakes and mudslides, little stones shot from lawnmower blades, death from above after plane crashes. There are other deaths too – or almost deaths, rope bruises from suicides by hanging, of freezing to death in the snow, surviving mortar fire, from the tragedy of droughts. The possibility that there could be another universe, unthinkable and unknown – that of the silent suffering and pleadings of trees – makes me treasure Von Ludwig more.

Café Morocco brews the finest coffee in the whole of OR Tambo International. The service is prompt, the café's carrot cake sinfully addictive, and its secluded position a voyeuristic paradise. Throngs can be observed from here, discreetly studied, speculations arrived at. Smokers are banished and fined, encouraged to seek coffee at other cafés that encourage slow suicides – assaults on lungs via tobacco smoke. Von Ludwig knows where to find me, knows our every meeting at the airport cannot but be at Café Morocco. He looks surprisingly agile for someone off a long-haul flight, smiles, arms wide open for that Von Ludwig hug: long and crushing.

Man from Stockholm! I charge.

Fellow Coffee Slave, I pledge my allegiance, he says. I smell a trace of sleep on his neck – but again, that confused scent can be anything.

Do tell, Fellow Slave, how was Stockholm?

Stockholm was a Swedish as ever, pleasant and laid back.

Tell me more, I say, almost choking on my coffee.

I will in a moment – but first things first …

Yes?

That friend of yours?

Friend?

Yes. That Michael K person.

What about him?

I spent a few days between Frankfurt and Zurich, picked up a copy of the book I told you about. I know you say he was oldish when you met him, but the book paints a picture of an early life, him as a young man, a troubled and nomadic life. I felt like someone was digging my innards out with a garden spade as I read – like someone had dropped an ice block down my back and left it there. I don't know if people like that exist any more, and I cannot for the life of me fathom how, if it was a biography, Coetzee managed to sketch such a lethal testament out of such a slippery character. The man you describe, the one you met and buried, doesn't sound like a particularly resourceful literary figure. It is remarkable that the laureate in the Land Cruiser extracted a whole life from a boulder.

He pauses very briefly, shrugs.

It is not entirely fair to say that, though, for the man in the book faces considerable challenges: the limitations of youth, a life during a time of war, the almost total absence of women in his life. You must watch it, my dear poet – a life such as K's cannot be emulated or desired, for it is or was K's nature to be who he was. He was born that way, with that cleft, the slow but not necessarily unremarkable mind, the instinct for a nomadic life, the urge for a life of seemingly eternal escapes. It is an impressive book, about a dramatic life, provided one maintains a balance in one's observation of K's life and how it is recorded on the page. There is, of course, also another dangerous possibility that it could be a different Michael. Who is to say that the one you buried is the one, if that possibility exists, that it is statistically possible for there to be at least one more pitiful-looking man with a cleft, with agrarian tendencies? I mean, such men should come from somewhere, and if they do, it should follow that there would be at least one more. It cannot be that only one is let loose into the universe, without even a best friend or distant cousin. Interestingly, it is quite vague and mischievous that your Land Cruiser man mentioned something about telepathic connection – between the writer and his creations, his characters, perhaps? – for that can be read in one or three ways.

He stirs his sugarless, milkless coffee, lays the spoon gently on the coaster. Proceeds.

One: it could mean that he has been around so many geniuses (some may say malcontents) of Michael K's ilk to have learnt everything there is to learn about them. Two: that he was indirectly telling you that he is a man of such artistic institution that he can decipher the inner workings of hearts of strangers. And three: that the telepathic connection could have been a cursory remark to confuse you ... Writers do that all the time, you know, to keep themselves in control.

In control of what?

Whatever they deem socially important, artistically valuable, says Von Ludwig.

You read the background and responses to the book – there should, surely, be survivors, next-of-kin scholars can trace to ask about this Michael K.

No, there aren't. Men such as those are like dew. They appear and vanish in silence. But you cannot accuse them of not having shown up. You don't have to understand them, it seems; maybe that is the trick: to appreciate them from afar. But then what would be the point of not learning anything from that which promises depth? And, of course, there is that contradiction: between a flesh-and-blood man who lived in a pyramid, as you say, and one immortalised in ink. It would have been ideal if he were not dead, if we could ask him: this man, Coetzee, says or claims there is a telepathic connection between the two of you, Michael. Is that true? What does he mean by that exactly? Do you know him? The whole thing might also be obscured by the entanglements of fame, for who is expected to answer to eight, eleven, twenty reporters at a funeral – and still provide accurate and insightful answers? We can't discard the fame: there is adequate proof that it is burdensome, imprisoning to those on whom it is bestowed. That is, famous people are always self-aware, have to fend off the slightest possibility of misunderstanding, to exist in a permanent state of a possibility to sudden or unforeseen combat.

I sleep badly, suffer what seems to be protests of the nerves. My urine burns and I have become prone to constipation (which translates into forty-minute Armageddons in the toilet), impatience and pleadings with knotted bowels that refuse to be moved. My eyes itch, from sleep deprivation I suppose, and my teeth have succumbed to a creamy yellow. I am despondent in the mornings – totally and utterly worthless in thought and deed, a nightmare my physician (the young Dr Wanner, Dr Z Wanner), who without touching the stethoscope, has warned me against.

Too much coffee, too little water, and an acute caffeine addiction. IBS – and it is called 'irritable bowel' for a reason – has never been friends with coffee, which explains the acid refluxes, the painful kidneys, the accelerated heart rate. You are not, technically speaking, ill, but I will nevertheless prescribe something mild to help your body flush out any toxins. Have you seen the urologist, as recommended?

No.

Why not?

I don't like the idea of strangers playing marbles with my testicles, and jamming gloved fingers up my butt, thank you very much.

The good doctor chuckles: I understand it is uncomfortable, but it is crucial that we do prostate screenings at least once a year.

Yes, yes, but is there no other way to do that without me feeling like I am being sodomised?

Not yet, no. There is no another way.

So what is the point of ploughing billions and billions of dollars into medical research if you cannot, as the medical fraternity, find practical ways of keeping gloved fingers out of people's anuses?

The doctor loses all professional composure and collapses with laughter.

You have a point, you have a point, he says between gales of laughter. I suppose some doctors must find it unpleasant too – having to pull aside people's thongs for examinations.

See? I say shaking his hand in solidarity. We talk about rain, about screenings for diabetes and high blood pressure, and I am made to confirm that the burning sensation down there has not and could not have resulted from manly preoccupations: an impressive euphemism short of accusing me of whoring. I caution myself that I might perhaps be too thin-skinned, that intrusions into bodies of others is nothing new, for if what Von Ludwig has read is true, Michael K did not seem to participate in or be bothered by a stranger gifting him an unsolicited hand job or oral pleasure on a beach. Maybe this is how I should think about it: be unaffected.

Coffee and Coke, I tell Dr Z. They are to blame. But this not completely true, for I, to stop him from referring me to a head doctor, do not tell him that someone has been calling my house at three in the morning and breathing into the phone. Just breathing and chewing gum. Not a word spoken. Not I hate you or you are a dead man, or watch your back. Just eerie and dangerous breathing. The sound of the newspaper dropping on the driveway in the morning startles me like artillery fire – jerks at knotted nerves causing me to reach for my handkerchief, to dab salty liquid from my eyes. Not quite tears – not yet – but a body succumbing to the power of emotions.

We meet at Melrose Arch for coffee – or rather, Von Ludwig downs coffee while I am humbled by the pedestrian pleasures of orange juice. Dr Z had been emphatic about the unintended brutalities of brewed coffee, and has made me suspicious but still indebted to roasted beans. The earthly airs of the Republic's well-off are in full swing: Porches and Rolls Royces parked on the street, meditative and drowsy babies ferried in imported French prams, and a suited young man (a banker, I imagine), without batting an eyelid, instructing whoever on the telephone to transfer nine hundred million for the Mexican Pipeline Project. Nine hundred million – in the hands of twenty-eight-year-olds, possibly commanding anxious grey heads about the inner workings of capitalism, saying: This is not some Mickey-Mouse investment, Alf. We're already running late and over budget, so I have no time or desire for fucking around! Only two tables away from Von Ludwig and me, this baby-faced but moustached dictator barely out of his diapers is raining the fear of God on his colleagues. It is impossible to know which of the well-groomed Melrose Coffee Joint patrons are human – if any of them conceal fur and tails under their Italian suits and frumpy dresses, if they, like K, have the remotest idea of restraint: the nobility of farming yielding a harvest of four and a half pumpkins, how to drink water from a looped teaspoon suspended on a string? What would the arrogant young man with the moustache have said if Michael K were to walk into the Melrose Coffee Joint, with its wooden floors and glass tables, its blood-red chairs, and request pumpkin soup?

I am assailed by the aromas of the Melrose Coffee Joint. Not that other coffee sanctuaries lack aroma, but the Melrose Coffee Joint lacks the deceits and trickery of restaurant design, is without the 'Staff Only' doors, without walls and suction fans to ward off smells, thus allowing momentary clouds of coffee steam to rise uninhibited into the air, intoxicating devotees with the bewitching aroma.

But the moustache tyrant is not done yet and fires: Dammit, Alfred! If that money is not burning wires to Mexico this very second, I am going to personally jam my hand into your butthole, all the way up, and yank your bladder out through your fucking arse. You have a lot of gall talking to your superior with that attitude! Hardly professional words – and the irony is completely lost on the moustache despot.

That, my friend, is poetry! Von Ludwig is grinning from ear to ear. Not only reading and hanging around poets, but wondering why some kisses are to the lips, others to the cheek, while some get planted on foreheads. Each kiss would require a different speed, duration, intensity – and therein, my dear sir, lies the sanctity of poetry. I thought I should tell you that.

I smile, nod.

He winks. The failure of poetry is when life humiliates us – treats us with disdain masquerading as difficulty. The senses become blunted, the world stale and colourless. Dancers miss steps, mist is mistaken for light rain, and bumblebees succumb to the toxins of fumigation. Butterflies vanish, composers of music weep into pillows. And other calamities of the curious and extreme kind.

I reach across the table and squeeze Von Ludwig's shoulder, and then before saying a word, reach for my fabric to restrain the sudden swirl of emotions that erupts out of nowhere.

Von Ludwig beckons the Melrose Coffee Joint manager to hand him his parcel, a parcel that turns out to be a gift: Bellow and James Baldwin first editions, the Bellow autographed. He cautions that the two gentlemen had refined gifts – those of peering into souls of humanity, with patience and a little danger, the danger of molten lava. He says I remind him of Moses Herzog, but I do not know who that is, and confess as much. You will find out soon enough, Von Ludwig tells me, and we will have all-day chats at the Botanical Gardens. So it has been forethought, prearranged, plotted. What a schemer, this Von Ludwig! He assures me there is great literary value in the two books, that I will be pleased to find portions of me scattered across their pages. Such graceful thoughtfulness, such investment in my decaying foundations hits me faster than I can reach for my handkerchief. I fumble for the strawberry-printed fabric to mop my face of emotion, tears that had already bolted, descending down my face, with speed and abandon. I fumble: pants pockets, front and rear. Jacket pockets left and right and jacket pockets inside left and right, shirt breast pocket – at which point Von Ludwig calmly asks: Can I be of assistance, sir?

My handkerchief, I say, averting my eyes.

A look of concern dashes across his face. He clears his throat. The handkerchief is in your hand, Miles.

We are joined by Boitumelo; perfect timing, which allows me to recompose myself in the company of the lovebirds.

I owe you an apology, says Von Ludwig, for in hindsight I realise that I might have contaminated and somewhat thwarted your poetic ambitions. I admit to be carried away, in over-personalising my views on and experiences with poets. The truth is, all poets I know and have known, famous as they are, remain but a small sample in an expansive field of other poets. As you are now aware, judging from poet friends we have hung with, the plain and sobering fact is that poets are just people – I mean, they love and scream and die and hate just like the rest of us. The difference is that they do it with a double mask: one part normal human and the other the mask of an artist. Now, art is not collected and stored and sold in buckets. Question is: where does it come from? God, if you are religious. But does God come to Melrose Coffee Joint, clap his hand to command attention and say: Listen, everybody! Or, Attention, poets! I have brought some sixty kilos of art, any takers? He does not, and has never done that. What does he do instead? He pretends that there are no poets, and shines through our senses a small light onto dance floors, onto sensual and crotch-imploding moves, on the delicate shoulders of tipsy women, on bumblebees parking and reversing out of tulips, on the mystery and dominance of vast open landscapes, on red lip stains on white coffee cups, on the million shades hinted at by moonlight from a young moon to a dirty yellow one, rising with grace and mystery. That small light, whatever it is and wherever it comes from, bounces off furious ocean waves, rests on virgin tongues, befriends the deadly beauty of certain swords. It lingers on harp strings, hides in the oversimplified white-wedding dreams of pubescent girls. That light hammers nails into coffins, gallops on horseback across tranquil streams, sniffs panties in closets and laundry baskets.

Of course, Von Ludwig and his Boitumelo are an admirable couple, admirable as any two love-soaked humans can be, for their fights can be epic, scorched-earth brawls dripping with historic judgements and future admonishing, wicked sneers and temper tantrums that make it hard to believe that the two are in love. I am witness to their moody withdrawals, cutting stares, their bordering-on-demented accusations and counter-accusations. I listen, too, to their heart-stopping reconciliations, am caught between them as friend, confidant and mediator, conflicted and burdened, sympathetic and bewildered. Neutrality is impossible, for all the weighty secrets with which I am entrusted, all the bliss and bile to which I am privy, the tiniest nuances of lingering hurts. And yet, Von Ludwig continues to state that Boitumelo is the 'starlight of a thousand twilights', a phrase much repeated, while Boitumelo confides that great pleasures are derived from intelligent conversations past midnight, that Von Ludwig's knowledge about the workings of the world is both impressive and sacred. She is to him 'a shameless demon in bed', and he to her 'the last of the sensual artists'. These things I know, continue to hear, embrace. The demon and her sensual artist, and poor old me with my strawberry-printed handkerchiefs. So inter-woven is our union of three that Boitumelo sees nothing wrong in sitting on my lap, kissing the crown of my head, and declaring me the most sensitive creature alive. She has done her bit to introduce me to at least two of her friends, Mary Anne and Matilda, delightful romantics, whom I kissed but never fondled.

It is peculiar that large portions of living can be consumed by way of coffee and verse, and yet it is indeed so because of the many coffee spots Von Ludwig and I frequent: the coffee havens of Menlo Park; coffee shots in motion from drive-through fast-food chains that never fail to usher foul brown-grey liquid far removed from coffee; the coffee-bean cremators in family-oriented restaurants of Saxonwold and Rivonia; the Melrose Coffee Joint and Morocco Coffees, of course; sidewalk coffee nests in Rosebank and Hyde Park, and our passing glances at coffee spots in the food courts at Johannesburg's malls. We are not unmindful that the coffee rituals conceal the formation of a brotherhood and, as is to be expected, many sleepless nights of staring at fan blades turning. There is a limit to the number of poems I can read, and I, when my mind gets weary, retreat to the balcony and, once there, attempt to, with a finger pointed at the night sky, draw an imaginary line that connects one star to another.

I, as much as I cherish our coffee pilgrimages, conversations that linger into the night, that are revisited or postponed, discoveries that birth speculation and uncertainties; as much as I look forward to the casting of doubt on established facts (how sure are we that trees don't feel pain?), I also succumb to jolts of conscience, at waiters shouldering eleven-hour shifts with a smile, wonder how exhausting such lives might be, the sheer force of will necessary to suppress emotion or dissent, to normalise potential eruptions of anger.

I notice that not all coffee connoisseurs come empathetic and well mannered, that some are intolerable and pompous brutes that should be lined up against a wall, coerced to recite the Bill of Rights and then shot. Von Ludwig always cautions me that it is impossible to account for the swine tendencies of others, that individual human consciences are not intended to carry such loads – and worse, that most if not all human relations are premised on one form of coercion or the other: the observance of military codes, how ward assistants cannot deny the surgeon a scalpel if so requested, just as motorists cannot drive through red traffic lights; how crippled planes can be denied landing authorisations because of the possibility that worse tragedies might unfold: the required runway not being available, occupied by a plane granted permission to rise to the night sky of Budapest, a plane in which passengers think of reunions with lovers and family, difficult work assignments in New York, oblivious to the occupants of the crippled plane on a wing and prayer, five hundred lives flashing in front of five hundred spooked people all shrieks and screams, in the claws of death and cremation via jet fuel.

The world, says Von Ludwig, cannot be without impositions against the will and sentiments of others, for no civilisation or social order would then be possible. That it was admirable that I felt the way I did, but that such oversensitivity was soul-denting and ultimately depressing. The grand irony is that such suppressions of free will happen in almost all democracies and major capitals around the world. This is the reason, perhaps, that some wombs nestle Michael Ks: to dilute, in inconsequential ways, the morbid twitches of human passions, expectations.

I take a leaf from a certain Moses Herzog, from a book recently gifted me by a good friend, and write:

Dear Mr President,

I have perhaps written a hundred versions of this letter in my head, the content and concerns of which changed according to prevailing national triumphs and ailments, thus delaying the arrival of the letter by at least two administrations. I intended to be deceased shortly after posting this letter, but have since taken that decision under review. Its current status is that of advanced gestation and meditative fog.

I hold no fanatical ideas or embarrassing addictions and was, until recently, in the employ of the state. Noting that presidential time is a rare and finite resource (I have yet to understand how heads of state calculate and account for time spent playing with cats and dogs, pets) – allow me, Sir, to puncture that which ails me. I am alarmed and appalled by the seeming mushrooming of two-legged rats in our government – humans who have decided to grow some tails and fur. Needless to say, I foresee calamity if an urgent solution is not found. I wish to risk an opinion and conclude that your office already knows (presidents and prime ministers have far-reaching eyes and ears) about the infestation of the two-legged creatures across the Republic, and wish to know how such knowledge coexists with your conscience.

My present circumstances are those of coffee addiction (hardly a narcotic), a dwindling pension and a soul contaminated by the aforesaid plague. Also, may I appeal to you, Your Excellency, to direct the ministry of Health to invest more in research as to the diagnosis and treatment procedures of selected afflictions: without the use of gloved hands. I have read somewhere that the Geneva Convention has ratified the use of gloves (or was it lubricants?) for such purposes, in respect of prisoners of war. This statute would be outdated in our time, surely.

I have, incidentally, inherited a Smith & Wesson from my slain father – who was a prominent member of your Party and also a long-serving administrator on the Johannesburg City Council. I am curious what procedures one follows after finding oneself a custodian of a legally procured firearm now held illegally. I have removed the said pistol from my father's house for safekeeping at mine, and have as yet not procured a safe, which I understand to be either strongly recommended or illegal for gun owners. Lastly, Excellency, I believe something needs to be done about the long working hours and compensation of waiters and waitresses, as they contribute directly to the health and wellbeing of the nation. A recently screened documentary on the SA Channel 40 suggests that pimps and escorts, by my calculations (reconfirmed with a calculator), make eight to eleven times the money paid to waiters and waitresses, not to mention teachers and nurses. That is, or should be, a moral outrage, surely? Just a thought.

Sincerely,

Miles M
41 Oak Street, Midrand, Johannesburg

PS. I was wondering the other evening whether your good office receives regular reports from the psychiatry institutes and their associated institutions across the provinces, and what picture, if you don't mind, those reports paint? To be specific, I am curious about what becomes of repressed anger emanating from turbulent historic and political transitions such as ours? In other words, what are the contemporary charms and sorrows of our Republic?

PPS. Pardon me, would I be correct to conclude that the current Minister of Defence still has intentions of being wedded, following the very public and embarrassing lapses by her former husband? Is she approachable, amenable to charming conversation? I would very much appreciate some guidance from you as her boss and cabinet colleague as to her views on coffee and poetic literature? Would she be keen to award eleven minutes of her busy schedule (if presidents have a moment to spare for their dogs surely ministers should have a little more?) to listen to a reclusive compatriot surviving on plant matter? I don't mean a herbivorous existence in its broadest definition here, but a vegetarian.

And:

There is a distinct possibility that trees are not as inanimate as we have always thought – in which case, they feel pain. What would the government's position be on this, bearing in mind the economic and moral implications of this proposition: forestry programmes, selected coffin and furniture manufacturing, no more wooden park benches; firewood would be unthinkable, and the face of architecture would change forever. Can you imagine a world without wooden flooring, sir?

Another letter, for an entirely different addressee, says:

Hello Amu,

There is something I have not told you about myself. I, in my younger days, twenty-four or thereabout, photographed models for a living, pointed varied lenses at an assortment of beauties for billboards and magazines. I was told I took iconic and timeless pictures, that only two pictures of mine were often enough to propel models to stardom, to earn me new model friends, hangers-on. There was no science or over-planning of anything, no mysterious method or rule book, no trick or formula: I simply let the lens follow and record the *soul* of the model. That was all. That she would be leaning against a beer crate or rusty 1970s' Chevrolet is secondary, inconsequential. It was the soul I photographed, how it moved through the model, how it settled in her eyes, how she breathed, how I focused on vulnerabilities most thought I couldn't sense. The way to photograph a beautiful woman, to ensure that the photograph is both captivating and timeless, is to imagine, assume her entire being to be the temporary beauty and perfection of a hailstone – because there is a fragility to hailstones, crystal beauty, but also rapid transformation: how they turn to unremarkable water puddles, pitiful, after having terrorised trees and broken windows. But being a lensman also depends on the type of photographer one chooses to be: those who dabble in nature and animals, specialists in mug shots, some with sensibilities to make architecture live, masters of the still images of sporting events, even photographers of a different kind – radiographers and X-ray people. There are other kinds, I'm sure, none of whom come close to portrait photographers, and more specifically, female model photographers: rendering in freeze frame, living, breathing, women, sought and kept and paid for their good looks. There are, technically speaking, many things wrong, or at least challenging in being this kind of lensman, challenges to do with proximity to an abundance of beauty in such contrasting and perplexing variations. The problem is this: such exposure, such consistent rendezvous with beautiful women numbs a man's senses to sense and see beauty, to appraise it, be moved by it. What becomes of a man desensitised from beauty, who cannot, even with manly instincts, wonder what attributes certain beauty categories have over others, which of the beauty scales would be worth dying for? It is strange, very strange, that though I am not completely blind to beautiful models I could not understand why some of my guests almost foamed at the mouth, so mercilessly contorted by these beautiful women with long necks and dangling earrings, out-of-reach conquests with magnetic eyes and guarded smiles. So it can be – and is indeed – very unpleasant to be blinded from seeing beauty, to be coerced by familiarity, to be almost indifferent to otherwise jaw-dropping looks, to brush off everything with a refrain: it is to be expected, models are *supposed* to be beautiful. It is in this refrain that much is lost, that there are burglaries and looting in the houses of love and desire, that beauty loses potency. It is much better, I assure you, for a man who photographs camels or wild monkeys, for even though he might possess great love for animals, it is very unlikely that he would lie awake nights on end pondering how to get their attention – and in my case, how best to shake them off whenever they attempt to cross professional lines. Such blurring of lines is seamless to some women, how they can elect to be prima donnas, to be entirely unreasonable, or become seductresses of the subtlest kind. Women are true masters in burdening or entrusting men with their wants and wishes, whether it be the banging of tables in demand of whatever or gentle coaxing, like how music connoisseurs gently lower or lift the needle onto or off a spinning record, the exactness of that action, planting the needle on a line to birth music.

And it was true: I was indeed the capturer, the lensman, of beautiful women. I cannot, however, say I was completely satisfied with the world of models and photographs. It fit like a glove, of course, but was inherently plagued by harmless and dormant falsehoods. Judging by the parents, the mothers and selected aunts, it was evident that some of the girls were never meant to be thin, that they would, with a typical life trajectory (marriage, children, divorce, remarriage, depressions and regrets) grow to their natural, God-given hips and girth, held in check by exercise and regimental starvations. Even the beauty was contaminated by falsehoods, the abundant access to things: clothes, make-up, accessories, shoes, fine wine and dining and handlers at no cost to them. Life in a bubble.

It is true to say that there was an accidental, erratic and unplanned spillage of emotions whenever a beautiful model removed herself from my soul-mapping sensibilities – when I couldn't connect my camera lens to what she was about, on a spiritual plane. I would shoot a hundred and one unsatisfactory pictures in multiple locations and know, even with a quick review on the digital screen, that something elementary and weighty was missing from the composition and life of those pictures. I believe, and have proven it to myself, that contrary to popular belief, photographs are living, breathing, affecting and instructive things that have the potential to arouse all sorts of reactions: anger, appreciation, yearning, surprise, shock, doubt, memory, irritation, love, mercy, deep thinking, and in some instances – especially photographs of models – little or overwhelming doses of desire. I have seen men and women stare at particular model pictures for the longest time, in Johannesburg's train stations and malls, at hairdressers, in doctors' rooms, oblivious to the fact that I, the originator of the photograph, was there, content that the heartbeat I implanted in each image was alive and well, beating, compelling people to smile and caress the magazine page, to frown in guarded admiration, to photograph the photograph with their smartphones.

Pictures without a heartbeat are stillborn, uninteresting, dead to the eye – a discomfort that had birthed my cooking for and hosting lone models for a light meal, watching cuisine and wine transform each of them from a cagey being to a bird, the darling of the modelling world; watching their awkward and sometimes crystal personalities light up in front of my very eyes, their souls – eyes covered with palms in embarrassment – lift their dresses to show me their nakedness. Yes. Souls are clothed things, so wary that most exist for lifetimes in their heavy coats and boots, never once allowing their skin to be seen. I am, once located, their heavy coats and boots discarded, able to shake hands with their souls, to reach for my Canon with a renewed understanding, a light path into the arable fields of my subject, into the depths of which I am able to plant a heart.

A friend tells me I must have been the luckiest man alive; I answer that he doesn't know what he's talking about. It is ruinous being in the company of such magnetic creatures, unhealthy for the soul to be so constantly stirred, to do shoot after shoot, be heated to boiling point by the sheer variety and intensities of beauty that pulse all over the Model Afrique Agency. I used to get all misty-eyed and tender-hearted after my shoots: all these faultless beauties who prove God exists, who often derailed and suffered meltdowns, who died premature and unnecessary deaths, who were marked from birth, as conquests, trophies to be collected, bandied about by men and fashion designers. I kept my feelings downplayed, buried, hidden.

Some lives end at thirteen seconds, some at an hour, still others end before they have begun – all those stillborn innocents fed to hospital incinerators, without name or purpose, without a single photograph, lifeless beings mined out of their mothers by means of vacuuming equipment and emergency surgeries, such muted violence that births devastating grief, on doctors and mothers alike. My life feels like that at times; when I lie in the hammock on the balcony, gazing at the night sky, and estimate the distance between the stars. I also wonder if some stars are hotter than others, if there is competition among them, an urge to embarrass and demean other coy and lesser stars. There are special evenings, when one to three shooting stars streak across the heavens, a smooth glide across the other stars, without a single collision. My heart threatens me with mock seizures, repressed groans. There are evenings when it aches, when I suffer shortness of breath. Von Ludwig suggests we stop swimming in coffee for a while and see if my panic attacks abate. I dread going to Dr Z – for the accusatory stare he jabs at me, the judgemental masquerading as doctorly concern. I think that of the many funerals I have attended, in cemeteries far and wide, I have yet to see a gravestone confirming and recording for posterity that anyone was killed by coffee. Worse, I think, the president has not bothered to respond to my letter, let alone a courtesy note to acknowledge receipt. I know he has the time, and though I cannot confirm he has a dog, it is a fact that he has the power to command people to do all manner of things for him, including the dictation of urgent letters. *Dear Mr M, I thank you for your letter dated such a date. I have directed so and so of such and such department to look into matters you raise, and my office will ensure XYZ and provide you with a response.* Something to that effect. There is, instead, palpable silence – which can be interpreted either as my being dismissed as a madman or taken for a clown. He certainly has the time: I see him on television inspecting the quality of cattle abattoirs, laying wreaths on gravesites from 1943, even attending a football match, which I am told lasts ninety minutes – more than enough time to respond to one letter. But I have Von Ludwig, a confidant of German origins and sensibilities, an eighth-generation Von Ludwig catapulted into German society by birth: German passport, German ex-wife (she wanted ship cruises and camping trips under starry nights while all he wanted was rendezvous with poets and jazz musicians), and the remains of other Von Ludwigs in German cemeteries. It is, many years after his divorce, happy season for Von Ludwig, it being the annual Joy of Jazz season, prompting jazz thirsts to be quenched at various venues: the Market Theatre, Bassline and the others; media types laden with cameras and notepads, ready to pontificate about jazz styles and lineages, for one-on-one interviews with elusive stars who have jetted in from Toronto and New Orleans, from Harlem, carrying in the sound of their horns and guitars, the wails and dirges of Mississippi, music that oozed from the veins of slaves. We are not here for the jazz, Von Ludwig and I, but for the Johannesburg Book Fair where we hop from one panel to the next like men demented – invigorated, scandalised, dazzled by the beauty of literary minds. There is a rumour that John Coetzee will read a paper by late afternoon, though no one seems confident enough to confirm if this is so, given that John is also, a quick website search reveals, scheduled for a panel discussion at the Budapest Culture Symposium today.

It was Maureen's last day yesterday. I did not expect that she would be that emotional, that she would hug my ageing carcass with such a force of life. I have learnt to detect a certain tingling of the eyeballs, and know that it is a warning: that I should reach for a handkerchief faster than usual, to minimise the embarrassment of weeping for no obvious reason. I have also learnt to dab my eyes much more gracefully, to compose myself, to be given away only by reddened eyes and a quavering lip.

You cry a lot, sir. Is something the matter with you? Maureen asked me before leaving.

No, no … I am all right.

You sure, sir?

I am. I am just tender-hearted, I suppose, born with certain valves and seals to counter emotional leaks missing.

She blushes.

Can I ask something of you?

Sure, she says.

These are supposed to be the best days of your life. Youth is a terrible thing to pawn away. Promise me you will have nothing to do with Brenton going forward.

I cannot promise you that, sir.

Why?

I love him. That's all. There is no explanation.

But …

He is much older, I know. I know about one other girl too. People think it is about money. If it were, why would I be scrubbing your floors?

So, is it love?

No. It is not only love. It is about life. And living. In the moment. That's all.

I see. I hear you. I will drive you to the taxi station then.

That's kind of you, but Brenton is already outside.

I think: maybe it is time I telephoned Models Afrique and picked up my Canon again. I still know some people there, still have something of a reputation. But I'm not sure whether my heart will survive the rigours of beautiful women, the constant stirring of the soul; or whether the coffee will suffocate and silence my weary heart.

I cannot say for certain when my implosion of conscience began, or whether it is in fact an implosion. It could have been no more than a temporary discomfort, propelled by I don't know what, finding expression in insomnia and a deafening need for solitude. Only neither life nor my professions permitted or offered solitary time, for photography is a trade of the eye and the imagination: that which the eye sees the mind has ambitions to frame; to capture experimentations with light and shadows, with unusual props (rusty period bicycles, feet dipped in outdoor aquariums, wartime aircraft abandoned on airstrips overgrown with shrubbery and grass). Photography did not and would not permit idleness, so I am unsure when my gauging of the soul began, the precise moment when the discomforts became mild irritations, that irritations became cumbersome distortions, persistent mental plagues. I think of it as delayed suffering, known to be imminent, yet suppressed and denied, through the admiration of beautiful women and pursuance of selected treasonous acts. A man was burnt alive a few days ago – on all fours and in flames, painted a foamy white with fire extinguishers on live television news, the world over. Another was stabbed to death in a muddy alley in Alexandra township – an argument over a cigarette or stalk sweet. One was a Mozambican whose fate my signature could have decided, when and how to stay in South Africa, for how long, one who had chosen to discard his own feelings in pursuit of safety, of understanding.

I love Johannesburg – like one loves and protects a fragile puppy, like one removes weeds from beds of blossoming tulips and roses. I am drawn to its formless danger, the lurking disquiets of a big city, by how minute and faceless I have become in the vast frontiers of its palaces and dungeons, how my stargazing crawls by unnoticed by my countrymen. There are other stargazers too, there must be, real stargazers who camp and live and thrive in the wild: lantern carriers and owners of books and celestial maps about the history and unknown charms in the world of stars. There must be true worshippers and disciples of these heavenly fires, these celestial corpses that have long died, exploded into trillions of graveyards that adorn the night skies. There seems, if I concentrate long enough, to be a certain secret that draws me to the stars: their ancient silence, their insistence on commanding attention without shouting from rooftops, unlike the shamelessness of thunder and rain, unaffected by their distance or determination. Stars are quiet – arrogant, maybe – but also of a particular crispness that takes refuge in every pore, every fragment of every hair that covers every slope and plane of the body. It is possible that Michael K is peering from behind the night clouds, content not to be bothered. He has seen the zealots and charlatans coming from miles away, preserved his soul in the most elementary of ways: the ways of silence. I concede: I was perhaps never formed to photograph people or to dabble in poetry to sign refugee reports that birth angst and strife.

It is disarming that even the proudest, profoundest and most private thoughts, embalmed by long evenings of quiet reflection and stargazing, are contaminated by the soundscapes of fucking and suburbia: groans and moans, exhilarated mating chants from young home owners ignorant of the principles of discreet pleasures; police or ambulance sirens, and the distant screech of car tyres in suicidal mode. I have learnt a remarkable squint: opening my eyes just enough to permit vision, an attempt to block out the excesses of city lights, which rob stars of their majesty. One by one faces come to me: beautiful faces, charmed faces, empathetic, doubtful, sinister, understanding faces, combative ones, vague faces – faces of people I have either known or observed.

The president has, almost two months later, not replied to my letter. It makes me wonder whether I misunderstood something, whether the world of politics is alien to that of conscience, if it is possible that the letter was lost by postal services, if a gloved hand opened it and read it out loud to a lunch shift of postal workers, to great laughter and mockery. I commune with the stars, seek their counsel as to whether I am being impatient, whether the matters I have asked of the president require months of thinking, even whole lifetimes? If he, the president, wishes to be advised – to request scrutiny of his thoughts and feelings from his inner circle: how personal and pure will his answer be if it has been influenced by the triumphs, fears and defeats of others?

Maybe it doesn't matter that I had once been a famous and much-lauded photographer, that I have, with my lens and passive lusts, derailed from the worlds of beautiful women to the worlds of bureaucratic slaughterhouses, to moral abattoirs. There I was slaughtered, alongside hundreds of thousands of others if not millions, for insisting on even the smallest crumbs of compassion. It all seems so distant now, now that I have discovered the seemingly infinite pleasures of stargazing, which though accidental at first, have grown to be quite commanding yearnings. It is a great irony that I have never allowed myself to be photographed – least of all by people who had convinced themselves that I had something to offer or say about the craft of emotive photographs. It is true that I am at times assailed by a tinge of sadness at my abandonment of the world of models – like a wooden boat anchored at some obscure small town and forgotten, its once-majestic and daring paintwork obliterated by the sun into peeling fragments of confused hues, the nails that hold it together rusted, its bottom scavenged by algae and time, its wood soaking up water in one, patient, futile surrender to decay and oblivion. I have not the courage nor the conviction to point lenses at strangers any more, and the more I think about it, the more it seems to me cowardly that one should direct effort only into that with which one's personality and talents fuse. That it was, in fact, quite natural to wonder about the inner workings of poets, though my latest gift (from Von Ludwig, of course), *The Financial and Erotic Lives of Deceased Poets*, is of little comfort in preserving the myths and mysteries that hang like dusty cobwebs over the lives and estates of dead poets.

As much as I have entertained the idea of procuring pumpkin seeds and retreating to faraway mountains in some faraway and never-before-seen place, I know that Michael K has already beaten me to it, that there would be nothing original about burrowing in holes and caves for withdrawals and solitude, even during poignant moments of suicide or meditation. That stargazing is too, I find, an old and tired passion: that there have as long as there have been stars also been eyes to watch them, minds to contemplate their arrangements, hearts to ponder their mysteries. That the life I have lived so far, ruined by compassion and good manners, could have been more eventful and colourful had I had the courage to frown at idiots and delinquents. But if Von Ludwig is right, it is possible for one to live without wants and worries, to traverse the earth with abundant private freedoms mistaken for purposeless excursions, to imagine the smell of stars, the beauty of their cold heat. That it is possible to admire and befriend the thoughts of poets, to – with a measure of fond admiration – drift in and out of sleep on the balcony, be awakened by Johannesburg showers cleansing one of the debris of unformed thoughts from decades past, of the dust of history and stains of personal failure choked into submission by raw ambition and manliness, erupting only in small, frequent, insistent protests intent on magnifying a precarious if not titanic battle, a tongue that has become incapable of licking wounds, that sits paralysed in reddened stupor.

There are, on nights that I forget the insect repellent, mosquito raids to contend with on the balcony, their whining from shins and chins, to ear tips and unsuspecting wrists. My bed is all breadcrumbs and poets, coffee and dairy stains, a fortress from which I command distant armies against the gnawing taunts of old age. The bladder is losing its alertness, bowel movement has become seasonal, and shaving such a chore that my face lies buried in thick forests of facial weeds. I am hopeless with pets, impatient with most humans, and exist in the arid and scorched landscapes of poetry and cold coffee, the occasional visit with Von Ludwig since his auto accident (I did not think he would make it), which I find to be tearful and draining, marked by long silences. The wit is still there, his eyes alert. The firm handshake too. Eighteen-year-old. Ran a traffic light at autobahn speeds. Ushered gloom into my life.

It occurs to me, suddenly and without forethought, that all I have felt, all those blunt and slicing emotions, all I have wrestled with – my small sorrows and blooming elations, doubts and fragile discoveries – have been nesting in me for all decades I mistook to be years of adulthood, of maturation of mind and of spirit. But it was not that; it never was. Like a wine cork I floated with false weight, of form but without the hardness demanded by the world – without real compulsive passions, devoid of grand protests. It is on nights like this, calm, warm with not an orphan of wind or breeze, that I submit to one fact: the horse that is my heart has galloped vast distances without horseshoes, four metal plates that give horse gallops their false power, their musicality, the unproven fact of warding off ghosts. It might not be desirable, but it is quite possible that the Smith & Wesson might not be too dramatic an idea in weighing one's options. And yet the stars keep glittering and, on clear nights, acquire a peculiar dominance: that of otherworldly and impossible-to-contemplate pricelessness. There will be no more letters to the president; the first was sent off in rage and haste – personality traits I have been dodging for the last thirty-nine years. But what does one do with hurt, with catastrophic disappointments, except rage and despair? I am not surprised that the letter was poorly drafted and perhaps ahead of its time, undesirable and ill considered even.

That I am at the edge of a cliff is true, already in the claws of flight, head first, even though humans were never meant to fly. The night skies have weaned me of doubt, though, ushered in something

I had searched for but never found: consciousness, that unparalleled power to be present, to feel. I reach for my handkerchief and, as I have perhaps millions of times, dab my eyes – shield them from the shame and despotic ambushes of sudden emotion. It threatens a downpour, but manages only a brisk drizzle, one that I let wet everything around me: the cold coffee, a newspaper bearing stale news, my socks and boots. Attempts at reading in the rain are futile, for the pages tear off Marechera and Jimmy Baldwin poetry like snowflakes, a scene witnessed by invisible but well-mannered thunder clearing its throat, and the most assured and determined erection not associated with fossils my age. I shall telephone Von Ludwig – tell him all about it, ask him what philosophical postulations are there around old men and their seasonal erections. To get his mind off things – off his pained and fractured bones screwed whole by orthopaedic surgeons. Von Ludwig has become less talkative, more reflective and, on selected days, so ponderous that he forgets I am at his bedside, holding his hand. Something has happened to that luminous mind; something has shifted. But Von Ludwig is determined. He telephones, insists we meet at the Café Morocco. I sit waiting – five minutes, then ten, twenty-five and thirty – until Von Ludwig's electric wheelchair meanders its way past throngs perhaps made up of airline pilots and cabin crews, of security personnel and cleaners shining floors, of taxi drivers and tourists. I realise how impossible it is to hide pity, and am determined not to reach for my handkerchief today. But Von Ludwig is all winces and hisses – and is, without his painkillers, in considerable pain. He should be in bed, strictly speaking, but he insists that he is hurt and not dead. Besides, he says, there are no worthier coffee slaves than he and I, that we should seriously consider establishing The Guild of Coffee Slaves – if no such corporation exists already.

I'm sorry I'm late. I had to wait for the tablets to kick in; my back felt like someone had pummelled it with a baseball bat. And my battery is flat, which renders cellphones useless. I also stopped at an obscure boutique on the retail floor and brought you a gift. Here, go ahead, open it.

A beret? For me?

Yes, a beret. The book says he wore a beret in his younger days.

He who? Jesus?

No, man. How could Jesus have worn a beret in 4BC? Berets were first worn only in the Bronze Age, my friend.

But you said *the book* ...

You can be slow sometimes. Not the Bible. Michael K. The book on Michael K.

Ah, the hare-lipped nomad in a beret. Some fashion statement. But why a beret for me?

It's a befitting accessory for powerful men: army generals and poets.

I'm going to look idiotic in this.

Wrong. It is not about you. It is what berets stand for – not what people think about them. Berets are cultural artefacts too. Even Michael K knew this – or, of course, it could have been a mindless accident. Brief pause. Have you started on the Marechera?

I was about to. But then the rain destroyed the book.

What happened?

I let the rain wet the book, then attempted to turn the pages.

You hated the book that much?

No. It seemed a worthy discovery.

I watch his eyes, search for the sparkle. There is none. So I continue, my feeble attempt to reignite a fire in them.

Books have been destroyed by fire for centuries now. Never by water. By rainwater. Because we always protect them – clutch them under the armpit, wrap them in a jersey, under an umbrella. We shield them from dust mites, from coffee stains, frown and rage when they get dog-eared. Isn't it stranger still that books, inanimate but weirdly animate things that can stir all manner of emotions, can even be considered dangerous, can amass reputations and disciples, somehow determine aspects of our worth in the universe (countless lies and false associations have been made with *Ulysses*, with *War and Peace*, with *Indaba, My Children*)? It is almost miraculous how many die off only to be resurrected, to be loved and worshipped anew, thought of and talked about. Toddlers die in the hands of devastated parents: why shouldn't books? You're a philosopher – think about it …

Our regular order arrives like clockwork: the best Kenyan coffee beans roasted (burnt?) to perfection, white liquid from the udders of cows, some brown sugar and carrot cake. I note a few familiar faces among the otherwise faceless throngs: a well-known newscaster of modest arrogance, a washed-out former model, a mascot for some chewing-gum company and that fatally disgraced politician. Among them, between a newspaper vendor and a television crew armed with news cameras and microphones, is John Coetzee.

I tell Von Ludwig this, point out the famous laureate.

You are drunk on coffee, scoffs Von Ludwig. That is not JMC.

But it *is*.

No, it isn't. Look closer. That would or could be his brother David, or another relative. Or a lookalike. The world is a big place, Miles, greater than you can ever imagine. Peopled with billions of variations of faces. Duplicates too. Even defective faces. Michael Ks.

THE POET

Many years have elapsed. I have not become a poet – at least not a practising one. Not yet anyway. Poetry continues to elude me in hurtful and embarrassing ways. Time and fate have savaged the Von Ludwig I knew, the philosophical and oozing-with-ideas Von Ludwig, replacing him with an almost mute cynic. Something went wrong with the surgery on both his knees, prompting – after a spirited fight with medics – a double amputation. He has two wheelchairs: one electric and the other a manual relic of old. Impatient motorists hoot at us: ageing assholes one called us, because we do not have the strength and agility of pubescents any more. We often have to endure abuse and irritations from our younger countrymen. And women.

My poetry diet has changed. A nonchalant Von Ludwig insists that I read poetry from home, that we have, now that he thinks about it, possibly started on the wrong foot with all those German and poets of other nations (yet he still cautions that art is universal), so we imbibe Mazisi Kunene in translation, get hammered by Lesego Rampolokeng with his thunderous assaults, his linguistic infernos, and dabble in some Keorapetse Kgositsile. True, poets are of the world, but they have flags to which some bear allegiance, have cemeteries at which beloved uncles and former lovers have been planted into the ground. Poets carry in their veins the lullabies and dirges of their people, the stains of their humanity. They are mental photographers of their nations: its landscapes, its scandals, its moments of valour and triumph. There resides in the heads of poets, says Von Ludwig, more emotion than thought, and more thoughts and silent speech in their hearts (a thinking heart!) – a reversal of the natural order of things that is erroneously and fleetingly called the madness of poets. When, I wonder, would such a strain of madness enter my heart?

Physical strength all but leaks out of me these days. I have pain everywhere: my joints ache, my vision is blurry, and my mouth is marked by a permanent saltiness. Those big liquid eyes of mine have become foggy, my grip and handshakes are limp and jittery, and my bladder has no intention of retaining urine, forcing me to drag my ageing carcass to the lavatory with humour and a sense of defeat. My mind is reasonably alert – one could even say good – before the harvest of tablets I feed on kick in. Medication for arthritis. For high blood pressure. Acute sinusitis. Seasonal migraines. My much-praised stride has been dealt a wicked blow and my posture has all but crumbled to a series of winces as I bend and straighten to breathe through and redirect jolts of pain. The surprising lucidity of my aged mind is no match for the sedative effects of some of the pills, leaving it smoky and muddled. It is as though veld fires ravage my brain, burning vast swatches of its landscape to soot, making it impossible for madness to lay its eggs, for them to hatch and bloom into melodious poetry songbirds with bright orange beaks. There are times when pockets of lucidity return, the promise of a few poetry lines that seem eminent yet still at great distances, when I reach for my crumbled and unironed handkerchief and dab my eyes tearful and a touch reddened, from aching bones and a foamy heart a heart with inadequate room for madness.

Money has all but run out and I have, save for the modest state pension, no other funds. The little I receive gets swallowed up by my medication, leaving me with enough to laugh mirthfully while immobilised by pain or sleep or drugs or all three. I sold Father's house to pay for an operation I needed; sold his car because I much preferred bicycles (the air that hits your face at speed, the muscle effort to enforce movement, the complete absence of fuel bills). But bicycles are for younger muscles – stronger joints – the reason my Raleigh is now rusting away in the garage with deflated tyres. With the little money I have left, I buy important things. Fruit. Jazz recordings. Poetry. I am pleasantly surprised at how my pauper life seems normal, desirable even. There are times when I feel detached from the world, but then those poetry nests emerge out of nowhere and dangle from my brain branches, their featherless chicks stillborn in almost-hatched eggs. How fragile those chicks, how quick they become food for scavengers: the ants of forgetfulness, the falcons of despair hovering above my nests, and the gale-force winds of mortality that threaten to end everything in a heartbeat.

I have read and reread the Michael K book twenty-three times in the last fifteen years or so. I sometimes sit and wonder: what does a man like Coetzee think about at three o'clock in the morning? Does he still write, for instance, or does he lie in bed sleepless, mulling his creations – Michael K, for instance, a nomadic simpleton-cum-fugitive (or is an *escapee* a more accurate term?) from Noël's work camp? I cannot tell which of the two Michaels is more interesting: the elusive one on the page or the flesh-and-blood recluse of Dust Island I knew briefly? Coetzee has not provided any explanations to his liaisons with Michael, so it remains a mystery which of the two Michaels he met first, which he holds in high regard. Von Ludwig says, with some authority, that the Michael K world stretches as far as Texas, for that is where (I am sure there are other places, other people sworn to secrecy?) some valuable documents have been deposited, entrusted, papers that will outlive Michael by a thousand years. That is the Nobel laureate's silent command to scholars of now and of the future, to piece together, build and shatter reputations on dim or insightful interpretations of how a creature such as Michael K is willed into existence: mocked and revered, a subject of literary and existential conversations on six continents. Rumour has it that Coetzee is rarely seen in public these days, that he has aged considerably, and that his withdrawal from public affairs has bestowed the ultimate crown of fame on him: mythical elusiveness. He has, to my mind at least, stirred the stars of the heavens with his liaisons and flirtations with the profound and obscure, conjured whole new galaxies at the centre of which Michael K seems the lone star: present but unreachable.

We sit on the patio of the Von Ludwig residence, reading and presiding over afternoon coffee. Von Ludwig says he has no desire to return to Germany; he relishes the perks of being a naturalised

South African, whatever those are. I tease him. What nation would he write for, if he were a poet: Germany or South Africa? He thinks, says: I don't know. The poetry will dictate.

He has asked me a pointed question, a question much repeated in various disguises and variations, an old question, asked at the infancy of our friendship some twenty or twenty-three years ago, a question of deceptive weight that when thought about, interrogated and an understanding reached, was and is a question that probes the very essence, the very nature of my being: What do you believe in? Gustav von Ludwig had asked me. I have since given the question much thought, have attempted to answer it as best I could, but always fell short of an exhaustive answer. I suspect I am a humanitarian at heart, I told him, a democrat, but I cannot say with any measure of finality if being humane and democratic is a personal ideology. I have, in attempting to answer Gustav, cautioned myself against artistic beliefs, for such a stance would be fraudulent and embarrassing; for I am yet to stumble upon a single line in my pilgrimage to becoming a poet. It might have seemed noble but not original if I had said I believed in human liberty: the sixteenth (maybe from the very beginnings of time) to twenty-first centuries have been bloodied by that ideal, the freedom of humankind. It is, therefore, not a great achievement to believe in human liberty, because that is one of the most primal of human instincts. Worse is the realisation that the world – and the place of humans in it – is so old that there is hardly anything completely new to speak of or to discover. Gustav is deeply touched by my answers, almost tearful, scratching the base of his stumps that itched mercilessly at times, says: You have not answered my question – that is, what it is that you believe in? You have, however, answered another question with aplomb, a question I haven't asked but you have, in your most private of private moments, answered: why it is taking you so long to become a poet? There is every conceivable answer in your wrong answer to what you believe in, but again, *wrong* is a relative word. The answer is this: you have the mind of a philosopher, my friend, a logical mind that thinks and does not necessarily talk to the heart. Conscience is, though important, an entirely different world in all of these poet inquests. Like I always say, you possess inadequate madness of the heart. But ... And pauses just briefly. But no one can say with absolute certainty that you won't wake up raging mad one day, poetry dripping like honey from your every pore.

I am old and sickly, Gustav.

So what? Some of the greatest works of literature were penned on deathbeds.

What would be the point? I would be in transition to other worlds and not concerned with poetry for its beauty, but as an imposition of my will on existence.

Aah, brilliant philosophical answer, albeit a mediocre artistic one: art is immune to old age, sir, lingering even after death. All you need is a heartbeat. Even if your arms and limbs had been sawed off, you can still request a pencil and a sheet of paper from your doctor or nurse or caregiver and dictate your poems to them. People – or, rather, some people – have great respect for the wishes of the dead or dying.

A single memory stands out: crystal clear to a point of being picturesque. So vivid is the memory that it somehow overpowers even my most potent tablets, rescues my mind from the fogginess of medical side effects. I am not sure if the memory is real or not, if it is not the result of an aged and decaying mind playing tricks, finding solace in its own illusions. In it Michael K sits on the rim of a concrete dam half dressed in washed-out brown slacks and no shirt, his bony chest reddened by the last stings of a setting sun. I can detect heat in his body, eminent perspiration if he continued to sit there observing lizards, bland and colourful reptiles raising curious heads to inspect the bigger creature arranging seedlings in various patterns on the rim of the dam wall. Birds hover overhead. Can they see or smell the seeds? An occasional bird perches on the far end of the dam, studies him, tiptoes towards him, its thoughts on the seedlings. Michael was never a feeder of birds. He is neither irritated nor intrigued by the bluish-pink bird and, continues to arrange his seeds without paying the animal the slightest acknowledgement. With an old windmill creaking overhead, Michael never once extended a hand of friendship to either the bird or lizards – but neither did he in any way threaten them. He seemed to have no interest whatsoever in living, breathing things – save for the seeds: dead and dried things that could sprout into life when conditions allowed, that could bloom and bear fruit, leave behind another collection of seeds for whom there is interest. A skew-nosed man arranging seeds on a concrete dam wall – with patience and purpose – so moved me that I was not offended that Michael K also failed to acknowledge *I* was there, completely ignored me like he had the bird and lizards. Maybe, I think, poetry is like that. Like seeds. At once dead and yet alive. That to extract that life from the seed, nurture it, one needs much more than patience, but a rarer kind of spiritual reawakening. The question is: where does one procure such a breed of spiritual consciousness, or is it only awarded to people with skew noses and dim minds? To arrange seed patterns on a dam wall, in total isolation and with such disregard for the world and life in it, and command such power that even birds and lizards come to pay their allegiance. There is something there, something great. I have but one final wish: that I live long enough to *know*, for certain, what it is.

ACKNOWLEDGEMENTS

I acknowledge and thank David Attwell with whom I briefly explored the fundamental nature and possibility of Michael K as an 'evolving' character. Thank you, David, for your time and audience. The essence and choices in the narrative are, however, entirely my own. All firing squads are, therefore, advised to seek me and leave David alone.

To my friend, brother: Malose Lekganyane, who knows and understands me. A great debt is owed to your humanity and laughter. Kgomo Mohwaduba!

I am also greatly indebted to the wonderful and selfless skills of Sean Fraser, my editor, and the timeless and evocative music of Simphiwe Dana, Mam' Busi Mhlongo and Nina Simone that formed the bedrock of the poetry motifs in this novel.

Lastly, and most importantly, it would be bad manners and uncouth behaviour not to acknowledge the source: thank you, John

Coetzee, for the gift and complexity of the original template from which I tried and hoped to be a decent artistic thief.

The following poetry extracts are used with permission of the publishers concerned:

Page 66: Extract from 'A Far Cry from Africa' by Derek Walcott (From *The Poetry of Derek Walcott: 1948–2013* by Derek Walcott, Faber and Faber, Ltd; and *Collected Poems: 1948–1984* by Derek Walcott, Farrar, Straus and Giroux).

Page 66: Extract from 'Poem XVII' by Pablo Neruda (From *The Essential Neruda* © 2004, 'Poem XVII' from Pablo Neruda's *Cien sonetos de amor*, translated by Mark Eisner. Reprinted with the permission of City Lights Books, www.citylights.com).